I0623283

Other Books from Inklings

Eclectic Writings Series Featuring Many Great Authors

Vol. 1 *Eclectically Carnal* compiled by Fern Brady and Chantell Renee
Vol. 2 *Eclectically Criminal* compiled by Fern Brady
Vol. 3 *Eclectically Vegas, Baby!* compiled by Fern Brady
Vol. 4 *Eclectically Cosmic* compiled by Fern Brady
Vol. 5 *Eclectically Heroic* compiled by Fern Brady, Kelly Colby, and
   Karina Winbigler

Books by Inklings Author, Ramon Del Villar

Payback, Book 1 in the Roberto Duran Series
Interpreters' Anatomy of a Civil Lawsuit, in English and Spanish

Books by Inklings Author, Meg Hafdahl

Twisted Reveries: Thirteen Tales of the Macabre
Twisted Reveries 2: Tales from Willoughby

Books by Inklings Author, Kelly Lynn Colby

Tarbin's True Heir

From Inklings International

Florilegio Poético del poeta Flavio Hinojosa, Jr.

From Inklings Children Division

The Smiley Face Blatoon by Lady Nefari Ydarb
   Available as a bilingual Spanish-English book
Picture Day, Ella! by Lady Nefari Ydarb
Vol. 1 *Perceptions: Special Needs* compiled by Fern Brady

ECLECTICALLY HEROIC

Eclectic Writings Series Vol. 5

Compiled by
**Fern Brady, Kelly Colby,
and Karina Winbigler**

Inklings Publishing

www.inklingspublishing.com

Eclectically Heroic: Eclectic Writings Series Vol. 5

Copyright © 2017 by Inklings Publishing

All rights reserved. Printed in the United States of America. No part of this book may be used or reproduced in any manner without written permission except in the case of brief quotations embodied in critical articles and reviews. For information, contact Inklings Publishing at inquiries@inklingspublishing.com.

If you purchased this book without a cover, you should be aware that it may have been stolen property and reported as "unsold and destroyed" to the publisher. In such cases, neither the authors nor the publisher received any payment for the "stripped book."

The scanning, uploading, and distributing of this book via the Internet or via any other means without the permission of the publisher is illegal and punishable by law. Please purchase only authorized e-books and do not participate in or encourage the electronic piracy of copyrighted materials. Your support of author rights is appreciated!

Compiled by Fern Brady, Kelly
      Colby, and Karina Winbigler
Copyedited/Formatted
      by D Tinker
Cover Art by Verstandt

ISBN: 978-1-944428-06-8 by Inklings Publishing
      http://inklingspublishing.com

First US Edition
Printed in the United States of America
21 20 19 18 17   1 2 3 4 5

To
the very real
heroes of the
Hurricane Harvey
catastrophe

CONTENTS

ACKNOWLEDGMENTS

As we worked to finalize this volume of our Eclectic Writings Series, the Texas Gulf Coast found itself imperiled by Hurricane Harvey. After making landfall, it became a tropical storm that sat pouring tremendous amounts of rain on Houston, Inklings Publishing's home. Stuck indoors, praying not to get flooded, we watched the news as the deluge unfolded. While there were some negative situations, overwhelmingly the horror of this storm system brought out the very best and most heroic elements of the people of the nation's fourth largest city.

While you sit and enjoy this collection of Eclectically Heroic tales, consider that right next door lives a real-life hero. In a time of natural disaster, your neighbor may well be the person that saves the day. And while they won't do it wearing spandex and a cape, it is these very real heroes that give us hope as we move forward as a society. Hope that if we can come together in such terrible times then we can find a way to come together for the greater good in not-so-terrible times.

As always, Fern Brady wishes to thank her Lord and Savior, the Great I Am, for his goodness and faithfulness. Above all else, it is His act of heroism on the cross that has made all the difference in her life. To her family, she sends all her love and gratitude for getting behind her in this crazy endeavor called running a book publishing business. To her four-legged friends, Arwen, Merlin, Grace, Coco, and Misty, she sends a ton of kisses and hugs and thanks for the smiles on dreary days they elicit from her.

Most especially, Inklings Publishing wishes to thank Kelly Lynn Colby and Karina Winbigler, who have come aboard on this journey and are the people responsible for this great volume. A special thanks to Dorothy Tinker for her fantastic editorial work on this volume and for being a fun and wonderful person to work with.

We hope you enjoy the fifth edition of our Eclectic Writings Series of anthologies. And stay tuned in 2018 for *Eclectically Magical*.

FORTUNE FAVORS THE KNAVE
STUART SUFFEL

"You think he's dead?" one rasping voice asked in a hoarse whisper.

"Dead? Only the living can die," another voice hissed back. "This one is the Devil's own. He can never die."

"Don't say that, Gurrand," a third voice sounded. "Else, what we doing here?"

I heard Gurrand, who was closest to me, spit. Their whispers sounded all the more tense in the dark, moonless night. I could almost reach out and touch them. But that could wait a little longer.

"We're here to assure our beloved princess that he's returned to the hell from whence he came!"

The other snorted. "You sure she'll pay us—our 'beloved' princess?"

"Well," answered Gurrand, "if she don't, she'll regret it. Now shut up and keep your wits about ye. Like I say, this one's the Devil's spawn, especially at night."

I admit, I did smile at this. It was true. Though born with but one eye, I was a much-feared assassin. One eye meant I was at a great disadvantage against any opponent in the broad light of day. So I did the majority of my killing at night, after years and years of sightless practice.

I did not unsheathe my sword, lest the sound alert my would-be-killers. I edged toward the spitter, Gurrand, and embraced him from behind. One of my hand's covered his mouth, the other clasped his sword hand. I closed my one eye, and we began to dance.

Gurrand's sword, under my assured guidance, cut through the leg of his nearest companion. The resulting screams alerted the third that something was amiss. I brought Gurrand's sword down hard on the injured party. The screams stopped. The third would-be killer spluttered.

"What—happening? Gurrand?"

I calculated that he was about six paces away. Too far. I loosened my grip on Gurrand's mouth. Gurrand called out a muffled, unintelligible cry. His accomplice drew closer and was about to speak, but Gurrand's sword denied him the privilege.

I took my dance partner's weapon from his hand and threw him to the ground. He cried out.

"Please—please. My lord knight—"

"No need to beg, good sir. I merely wish to ask you some questions," I reassured him.

I believe he assumed I was going to spare his life afterward, poor fool.

It seemed I had been declared dead, and Princess Sasha's new pony, Knight Yourik, the very one I had witnessed her corral the previous evening, was to be made King's First Arm in my stead.

If only I had killed him there and then, when I had seen him in her chambers, instead of retreating to the wine cellar in dismay. That was my first mistake. Riding while drunk was my second.

My head throbbed like a wasp-stung thumb. I had awoken some hours earlier under an oak tree with several mules kicking the inside of my skull and a stomach full of ill. After throwing up what felt like a thousand meals, I had searched for my trusty steed, in vain. I surmised he had most likely returned to the king's stables by himself, probably grinning all the way there.

I, Paradar Gallsan of Orum, the great Demon Knight, had become a laughing stock. Usurped, not only in royal favor but in the royal bedroom as well. A double disgrace. From future king to hunted outcast. Oh, how the mighty had fallen. She had used me, my princess. Used me and then cast me aside. She was not but ten years older than me, yet she was truly centuries my senior.

Part of me did admire her expediency. A bigger part of me craved revenge. I looked down at the three lifeless bodies of my attackers and realized my mistake. When these fools didn't return to the palace, she would know I still lived. I had let my heart override my head. Now she would only up the purse she had promised these three to other hopeful killers. She might even persuade those few noble-born who remained alive to hunt me down. They certainly wouldn't need much encouragement.

But then Gurrand's words came to mind. *This one is the Devil's own. He can never die.* I grinned. If the citizenry of Balaam regarded me as Devil-born, how much more would they fear an angry Devil-monster who simply would not die.

One disadvantage of wearing an eye patch was just how easily identifiable you were. For my upcoming performance, it was ideal. I dressed Gurrand up in my clothes, complete with the eye patch. He was not my exact size and stature, but that would make little difference in the darkness.

I found my attacker's horses nearby and placed him across one. I arrived outside the palace an hour later, my puppet in tow.

I hauled Gurrand's body onto a wooden stake, leaving his arms free to maneuver. The sky was a murky darkness, the moon submerged in heavy cloud. A perfect stage. I stood behind the corpse, placing my own sword in his hand. I checked that the rope holding the corpse to the stake could be quickly released. It could. I tucked a soaking wet rag under my belt and then lit the torch beside my life-sized scarecrow, cleared my voice, and gave out a mighty shout.

"Citizens of Balaam. Behold your judge and executioner."

I hadn't been sure of what to shout exactly, but I kind of liked the sound of that sentence. Feeding the fears of the citizens of Balaam would not take too much effort.

For a moment, nothing happened. Then the sentries my beloved had ordered to the walls since my death, lit up a torch. "Who goes there?" a voice called out.

I heard the nervousness in the voice and grinned. "It is I, Lord of Night, Savior of Balaam, First Arm of King Balfern. I have come this night to rid you of evil."

I heard a scurrying across the wall balustrade. Voices spoke in subdued tones. After a short while, a willowy figure appeared on the wall. It was my sweet princess. She whispered to the night's guard captain. He cleared his throat. "The only evil here this night is *you*. Go now, or we shall unleash hell upon you."

I raised up Gurrand's arm, brandishing the sword as best I could make him. "Give the demon witch to me, or you shall indeed know hell." I almost laughed but managed to keep from doing so. I watched with glee as the captain and my fair princess frantically exchanged words.

"There is but one demon here," the captain offered. "Lay down your sword, Lord Demon, and Her Royal Highness shall offer you mercy."

This time I did laugh, but I kept it low. I lifted the sword in Gurrand's hand as high as I could. "Never!"

An instant later, the captain gestured, and a flurry of arrows sailed through the air. They thumped into Gurrand's body with a resounding punch. A moment of silence held, and then the balustrade broke into a round of cheering. I allowed a few moments to pass before calling out.

"Citizens of Balaam, you show me dishonor. I say to you, give me the demon witch you call Highness, or you shall know true hell."

I could feel the panic spread along the wall. But in fairness to the captain, he held firm. "Archers, ready." The archers obliged. "Release," the captain called out.

Again, the thump of the arrows rang across the open ground. This time a few of the arrows made contact with poor Gurrand's neck, slicing it through and causing the head to loll to one side, though it was still attached to his shoulders. Another cheer went up.

Again, I waited for a moment or two, then threw some dirt on the torch beside me to dampen its light a little. I lifted the badly damaged corpse, quickly kicking the stake to the ground. I gently lifted the head upright, placed my body fully behind Gurrand's, and proceeded to walk the corpse forward about ten paces, away from the torchlight. I could hear every frightened gasp as I moved toward the wall. The most they would be able to see was an outline of Gurrand's lifeless corpse.

I stopped. "Listen to me, good citizens of Balaam. It is not *your* souls I seek. It is that devious witch you call princess. If she is not placed outside the palace gates within the hour, I shall return at first light. I shall raze these walls to the ground. I shall trample all within. I shall send you all to hell. You have been warned." I pulled the wet rag from out of my belt and threw it behind me. It landed on the torch perfectly, extinguishing it completely. Now, in total darkness, I quickly hoisted my mutilated puppet across my shoulders, retraced my steps, grabbed the stake and the wet rag with my free hand, and moved as fast as I could away from the palace walls.

I waited in the underbrush some distance away to see if anyone would leave the palace to confront this undead demon who had threatened them so fiercely. None did. None, that is, until exactly one hour later. The four knights who exited the palace were accompanied by a furious, defiant-looking princess. But her defiance did not unlock her bound wrists or the hearts of those who dumped her so unceremoniously onto the cold, wet earth before scampering back inside the palace walls. I almost pitied her.

Almost.

The cave was one I had found during my turnip-eating days, long before I had entered the palace guard service to eventually become Princess Sasha's much-feared favorite. It was small but well concealed from the world. It filled with groundwater by day, but at night it was dry enough to sleep in, at least for those with no other choices.

I watched with satisfaction as she struggled against her binds. Her fiery green eyes flashed in anger. She was stunning, even in anger. Especially in anger.

"They were certainly thorough," I quipped, nodding to her binds. "Wasn't that Knight Yourik amongst them? Bit of a lovers' tiff, was there?"

She cursed under her breath. Even then, I desired her. I was never going to hurt her. I couldn't. Tease her, yes. Maybe scare her a little, if such a thing was possible. But hurt her? No. I may even have won her back. Some more teasing, then a few hours of—

"You're just like your father," she growled. My expression of shock pleased her. She laughed. "Yes, he was a ruthless, idiotic vagabond, too."

I managed to stutter a question. Something like, "How . . . ?"

She laughed again. It was not a pleasant laugh. "We were lovers, he and I. Or rather, he was my plaything. When I tired of him, I told my father he'd attacked me."

I looked at her for a long time. I could see she was telling the truth. Finally, I spoke. "You . . . had my father executed?"

She nodded. "Others are repulsed by the Accursed. I am drawn to them. But your father was too weak to grasp his destiny—too loyal to a decrepit crown." She frowned. "Don't be a fool, like your father was. You have great potential. The king is a weak, old man. I tell you, the throne is yours. I can give it to you. Untie me. Unite with me, and we shall return to the palace triumphant. You, the Demon King. Me, your loving queen."

I wasn't sure if it was the word *loving* that caused my stomach to heave, or the depth of her evil. I sat down, my head spinning.

Demon King. Accursed.

These were not words of my choosing.

My home village came to mind, the day my father swung from a makeshift gallows in the village square. The looks I had received from my fellow citizens were not looks of pity. They were glares of contempt.

"Paradar," Princess Sasha continued, "my love . . ."

I stared at her. "Do not—do not call me that."

"Lord Demon . . ."

"Do not call me that, either!" I stood up and began to pace. I stopped. "My mother . . ."

"A terrible tragedy—"

"Denounced as a witch! Burned alive upon the very gallows from which my father had swung but hours earlier!" I sat down again, my stomach in knots. "And my poor grandfather—"

"A great hero. A most loyal and fearsome warrior. You have his blood, my lord. You—"

"Died of heartache. They buried him in a pauper's grave . . . stitched a wooden block to the stump of his right arm in place of a hand. A hand he lost in service to the king!"

"My lord, tradition dictates . . . lest he might rise from the grave as a demon and wreak havoc among the citizenry. Foolish nonsense, of course. Yet such superstitious fears shall give us power over them. Don't you see that? We shall rule with—"

"I blamed my father. My own father . . ."

"Untie me, my love. Let us—"

"You! You created me! You made me the monster I am!" I shouted.

"We are all created by circumstances, my love. But we are made great by our deeds." She raised her hands into the air. "Untie me, my love. Untie me, and we shall—"

I stared at her. "I said, do not call me that. Do not call me *love*. You used me. Like you use all. You do not know the meaning of love!"

"Untie me, you fool! Untie me and rot here, in this filthy cave, if you haven't the sense to heed my wisdom!"

I stood up and took out my long knife. Her eyes flashed with fear. I reached out and sliced open her bonds.

Wisdom. The world was full of wisdom. "Go," I said.

She glared at me. I collapsed back into a sitting position, still somewhat dazed. As she passed me, she whispered, "Fool." I did not respond but averted my eyes. I could not bear to even look at her. Thankfully, I did glimpse her reflection in the small pool. I moved my head away from the blow just in time. The rock she had clutched in her hands carried her forward. Her head hit the stone floor with a thud.

Almost immediately, blood streamed from her mouth and her eyes glazed over. She was dead.

Sometime after, I found myself entering the palace walls. I did not know where else to go. All vanished upon my approach. Cries of "Undead" and "Demon" filled the air. I ignored them, too tired to care.

I went to my rooms and collapsed onto my once-royal bed. Some hours later, a knock came on my door. I opened it to a terrified-looking herald. "O-our gracious king, m-my lord. He requests your presence."

A while later, I entered the king's private chambers, unaccompanied. King Balfern stared at me. His eyes were grey and murky.

"Reinar?"

He was no more than sixty, but he looked closer to eighty. I shook my head. "No, my King. My name is Paradar. Paradar Gallsan. Of Orum."

He gestured me forward. When I drew close, he whispered, "Is she dead?"

"A tragic accident, my King . . ." I muttered feebly.

He nodded. "She killed him, you know. Sasha did."

I froze. Was he referring to my father? Did he hope to absolve himself?

He whispered again, his head bobbing as he spoke. "Pushed him into the swamp when he was but ten years old. Watched him drown."

I reeled in shock. He was talking about the young Prince Reinar. Sasha had murdered her own brother?

"No proof, of course," he continued. "But I know. I've always known." His eyes grew clearer; his bobbing head came to a rest. "I am no fool, Paradar of Orum, though many think otherwise." I gave a weak gesture. He nodded back. "Yet no man, king or no, can take his daughter's life. Not even a daughter as evil as mine."

I said nothing.

"You have wreaked much havoc, good knight," he said. "Decimated our ranks of noble-born, and all at the behest of the Princess Sasha."

"My King . . ."

He gestured for silence. "The game is played. The rules, we make along the way. You think they give kingdoms to those who ask politely?"

He grinned, and I could not help but grin back.

The king's eyes narrowed. His head began to bob up and down again. "Your eye. It is gone?"

"Yes, my King."

"Another tragic accident?"

"One of birth, my King."

King Balfern smiled. "Not all tragedies are accidents, my boy. Just as not all accidents, are tragic." His eyes twinkled. "One of the Accursed . . ."

"Indeed, my King."

"He had a lame foot, my son. Did you know that?"

I shook my head.

"Yes. Lame in body, but not in soul. You are a hero, Knight Paradar of Orum. To me, and to many. And soon, very soon, you shall be king. King over a kingdom of superstitious, backward, petty fools. Is this truly what you want?"

I looked beyond the king's shoulder to the full-length windows that led out to the palace courtyard—out to the nearby fields and villages beyond, to the faraway rambling hills and many soft valleys that made up the Kingdom of Balaam.

In my mind, I heard the creak of a swinging gallows rope, made taut by the weight of ruthless ambition. I inhaled the smell of burning flesh from the body of a hapless young mother. I witnessed the sight of a once-strong old man lowered into a pauper's grave, a wooden stake in place of a hand, fastened there by years of fear, fanaticism, and hate-filled prejudice.

The words of Princess Sasha came to me. *We are all created by circumstances, my love. But we are made great by our deeds.*

Strange, such wisdom from one so devoid of insight.

Gradually, I focused my one eye on the old man sitting before me. I smiled as I spoke.

"It is, my King. It most truly is."

GALLOP
CATHY CLAY

Fairy tale be damned at
the sight of you breaking
through stable doors.

Even bridled, something of your essence,
thank God, remains untamed.
Upon your back, I find refuge.
My burdens grow light,
cares are liberated, and
sorrows gain perspective.

Whether saddled or bare, in
your trot lie treasure and truth.
Astride your canter reigns
clarity and consolation.
In your gallop, goodness
and glory dwell.

A good mount is a mount
manifest by many names.
Appaloosa—Faith,
Friesian—Valor,
Lusitano—Friend.
You, you, you . . .
four-legged deity

just outside paradise.
Under the weight of
your mighty, sacred hooves,
my demons are crushed asunder.
Above your sunlight-dappled mane,
my Lazarus dreams stir once again.

Stallion—
you salvaged what was
left of this renegade,
and kept her for yourself.

You swam the indigo pools
of my soul to find the long
forgotten fortune of joy!
The black path wrought by
my misguided passions
was sanctified by your prance.
To behold you at play in pasture,
awakens the memory of my dance.

Gelding or mare,
you slow when I am weary,
quicken when I am bold.
Equus caballus, I see your wings.
You see my soul.

MASTER OF MY WORLD
DOROTHY TINKER

The rainforest is quiet as I amble slowly into the small town of
Canazel. I keep my head low as I wander the dirt streets, lipping
curiously at the tufts of grass that border them. I lack a rider, but it
won't matter. Towns like this allow their horses free reign. After all,
what horse who has known even the slightest presence of a Mago
Animal would willingly enter the unknown of the wild rainforest
without an humano?

I snort softly. *One with a purpose.*

As I slowly explore the town, gentle light begins to suffuse the air
beneath the high canopy. The singing voices of birds begin to rise,
accompanied by the screams and cries of more land-bound animales.
Around me, humanos begin to step from their abodes, many greeting
each other before beginning their daily tasks.

The brush of a hand against my shoulder startles me, and I flick my
tail against my flank. When I turn to glare at the humano who
touched me, though, he's already wandering away with a murmured
greeting.

Easy, Mundomía. They have no reason to guess your purpose.

I huff but accept the assurance of the presence in my mind. This isn't the first time Maestro has sent me into a village or town, and he's never steered me wrong before.

Brief brushes and quick greetings turn out to be common in this town, and I relax more and more as each humano turns away afterward. A couple of them even offer a piece of fruit or vegetable, which I take happily.

One such piece is offered by a young boy around midmorning. I take the carrot with pleasure; it's stubby, but the scent hints at a fullness of flavor that is rare. Closing my eyes, I relish the flavor and ask Maestro if he can find the source when he arrives.

The presence in my mind is murmuring an affirmative when a small, light pressure against my nose makes me jerk my head backward. Opening my eyes, I stare at the boy who gave me the carrot. Dark, shaggy hair frames his warmly colored skin and bright blue eyes, and he offers a gentle smile.

"I've never seen you before," he nickers.

Nickers. In the tongue of the animales.

My heart thumps heavily within my chest and my breathing speeds up. I'm not supposed to attract the attention of the local Magos Animales. Maestro will be upset and—

Cálmate, belleza. I am not angry. The boy is young yet. I doubt he can sense anything.

But, Maestro, I think, yet the presence in my mind is adamant.

Remain calm, belleza. Our purpose has not been compromised.

I stare at the boy, hesitating. Maestro has never steered me wrong, but there's something worrisome about this gentle boy.

When the presence in my mind grows heavier, I release an even heavier breath and press my snout back against the boy's hand. *Sí, Maestro.*

"That's it," the boy nickers soothingly, stroking his hand lightly up and down my snout. *"I won't hurt you."* The idea that such a small creature could hurt me makes me snort, but the boy ignores the sound. *"You and your owner must be visiting. Has your owner found you any accommodations for your stay?"*

I nicker warily. *"What do you mean, accommodations?"*

Surprisingly, the boy grins. *"Sí, you're definitely not from Canazel. My familia takes care of most of the horses in town."* He swings one arm out behind him and gives a small bow. *"If you'll follow me, I can show you the way."*

I hesitate, but Maestro's presence grows heavy in my mind once more. *Go with him, Mundomía. If he's right and his familia does care for all the horses in town, that is where you need to be.*

I huff out a soft agreement and slowly follow the boy down the street.

As it turns out, the boy, Tomás Cabita, is well-known throughout the entire town. It seems like we're greeted by every humano we pass. Even the animales lift their heads to acknowledge our passing, though their gazes often linger longer on me than on Tomás. I nicker a greeting to each animal, which then feigns indifference as we pass.

"Here we are!" Tomás finally declares, stopping in front of a large wooden building with a wide, open doorway, through which warm light spills. *"Taberna Cabita!"*

I eye the lit interior. *"Taberna? Sounds like an establishment for humanos."*

Tomás grins widely. *"Not at all. My familia has been Magos Animales for as long as the town can remember. Here, we make the animales happy, not the humanos."*

I nicker curiously. *"Does Maes—my owner need to be here for me to find . . . accommodations?"* I silently curse myself for the slip, but Maestro remains silent in my mind.

"Not at all," Tomás answers cheerfully. Turning toward the open doorway, he switches to the humano tongue of Pecalini and shouts, "Madre! Papá! I found a visitor!"

"Not so loud, Tomi," a darkly colored mujer chastises as she wanders from the building's entrance. "You know some of the animales are just now getting to sleep."

Tomás crosses his arms and pouts. "My nombre's Tomás, Madre, not Tomi."

The mujer snorts. "Until you can learn to mind your manners, I will continue to call you Tomi." She turns to me, and her eyes soften. "Now, let's get your new amiga cleaned up and settled." She glances past us and adds, "Will her owner be able to find her?"

I nicker an affirmative, and Tomás snorts. "Of course, Madre! All he has to do is ask anyone in town, and he'll know where to find her."

The mujer frowns at Tomás. "As long as she is sure he will."

I nicker again. "She *is*, Madre," Tomás insists.

The mujer nods. "Very well." Turning to me, she adds, "I'm Vera Cabita. I may not be a Mago Animal, but I will do everything I can to make your stay here in Canazel a pleasant one. If you'll follow me . . . ?"

Vera leads me into the building's warmly lit interior. The space is wide and open. The right side is divided into several open stall-like structures, many of which are occupied by sleeping animales— horses, cats, rodents, and even a large snake that I eye curiously before turning toward the opposite side. The length of the left wall is laid out with water troughs and various types of food—hay, alfalfa, fruits, and vegetables. I wonder briefly if they have any more of those richly flavored carrots.

"Ah! Tomás!" calls a voice from farther into the space. "Did you manage to find Terrablanca or Cuellor?"

Tomás shakes his head. "No, Papá, but I found a new visitor. I don't think her owner knew about Taberna Cabita, so I thought I'd bring her over."

An hombre with gray-flecked dark hair and warmly colored skin strides from the far side of the room, which I suddenly realize is occupied by criaturas I didn't expect to see in an humano town—two of the winged horse race known as equavians and a pardavian, which looks like a winged jaguar.

I'm so distracted by the three criaturas mágicas that I miss the older Cabita's next words. It isn't until a hand runs along my left side that I pull my gaze from the three criaturas and turn my head to eye the hombre.

"A bit odd that she doesn't have any tack." Glancing at Tomás, he adds, "Does she have an owner?"

"Sí, I do," I snort sharply. *"And I would appreciate it if you asked me such questions, not your hijo."*

The hombre blinks before chuckling and shaking his head. *"My apologies, señorita,"* he nickers, slipping into the tongue of the animales.

"Not all of the animales who come under our care enjoy speaking with Magos Animales. Tomás can usually make amigos where others of us cannot."

I toss my head and glance at the boy. *"I can believe that,"* I answer, which earns a grin from the boy. *"But I have never been one to shy away from a mago."*

The hombre nods and offers a warm smile. *"Very well. Then why don't we get you settled and show you how we care for animales here at Taberna Cabita?"*

By the time evening rolls around and darkness drapes over the town, I have settled on the floor of the open stall beside the large snake's. It's lined with a thick layer of grasses, providing a cushioning effect that will lull me to sleep if I allow it to. In front of me, the two equavians and the pardavian converse softly in a mixture of nickers, growls, and trills that I pay only the barest of attention to. Even the large snake, despite the softly hissed greeting he offered earlier, is of little concern.

Instead, I focus on my reason for coming to this town in the first place. A good brushing, delicious food, and a tantalizing place to rest are all wonderful, but I can't let myself be distracted from the purpose Maestro has set me.

Settling my body into stillness, I tug at a part of myself that's always present, a subtle warmth that's as much me as it is Maestro. The warmth has been seeping out since I entered the town, but now I purposefully reach out with it, first sensing and then actively touching the other animales who fill Taberna Cabita.

Here is a large, coiled form filled with strength and lazy hunger. Here are heavy wings and claws and powerful haunches. Here, lithe, hot observance. Here, small, squirming anxiety. Here, subdued speed. Here, patience and loyalty.

I sense and touch all of these and more. I don't name the animales as the power I wield encircles them. I only acknowledge *what* they are and how I can best convince them to my purpose.

Once the power has found and touched every animal within the building, I reach out into the remainder of the town. Many I touch feel familiar, and their essences easily accept the influence they have already acknowledged previously.

I lose myself in the task, touching, encircling, and persuading the animales of Canazel to my purpose.

I'm still lost in the power when the beloved presence in my mind stirs. Gladness thrills through me; Maestro is on his way! I settle even more heavily into the power to await his orders.

I know the moment Maestro enters Canazel. As the town wakes for a new day, the animales I first encountered upon entering the town stir beneath my touch and follow the new presence with their eyes. The awareness of his presence sweeps like a wave through the town, an undercurrent that most of the humanos would not be able to recognize.

The Cabitas, however, are not most humanos. Amid the blanket of subtle power I have spread across the town, the familia of Magos Animales shines like glaring beacons—all ten of them. I didn't touch them with my power, but I can still sense them and so I know exactly when the first one notices Maestro.

I wish I could witness the interaction between the townspeople and Maestro, but my place is here for now. Besides, the interactions are almost always the same: either the people recognized Maestro's authority immediately and give him what he wants, or I teach them the truth of his authority and they eventually give in.

Even the presence of the Cabitas cannot change that routine.

When the first humano attacks Maestro, three hounds attack him. Two more attack a second, and two horses, who haven't been in Taberna Cabita since I arrived, restrain the next two.

At this point, the large snake slithers out of his stall, heading toward Taberna Cabita's entrance, and the equavians and pardavian quickly follow.

Several more minutes of violence pass, and I might have to acknowledge that this is a particularly stubborn town.

Or simply overconfident? Perhaps they expect their ten Magos Animales to surpass Maestro in power?

"What are you doing?"

My head jerks upright. Bright blue eyes stare at me from the entrance of the open stall, while small, dark hands clutch at the wooden frame.

"What do you mean?"

"What do I—you're sending the animales out to attack my amigos! My familia! Why?"

I huff. *"I wouldn't have to if the townspeople would listen to my maestro and do as he asks."*

Tomás's hands tighten on the frame of the stall's entrance. *"Do as he asks? What could he possibly ask of us that would justify attacking us with our own animales?"*

I tilt my head and eye the boy. *"Maestro needs something. I may not know what he needs from your town in particular, but I don't need to, to do what he asks of me."*

"To do what he asks of you?" Tomás repeated. His eyes grow dark, and he shakes his head slowly from side to side. *"You don't even care?"*

"Care about what?"

Tomás hisses like the snake that was previously in the next stall over. *"About the deaths! About the violence! About what's right!"*

I remain silent at first, half my mind on the power I still wield at Maestro's direction. The boy speaks of things he can't understand. There would be no death, no violence, if the townspeople would only accept Maestro's authority. And it's only right that I do as he asks. It's his power I wield, his authority I enforce.

When I say as much, Tomás shakes his head again and backs away from the stall. *"Malos. Both of you. I thought—I brought you into my familia's home. I cleaned you up and fed you. And you don't even care! You're just as bad as he is. Just as evil!"*

He spins around then and runs for the building's entrance. As he does, power rises around him, reaching out more strongly than I would have expected. It touches and tugs at me, and I suddenly recognize what I didn't before: the boy may be young, but he is powerful and his Animales Poderes are horses.

He'll never influence me, but the other horses . . .

I clamber up to all fours and leap after the boy. *Can't let him leave! Can't let him leave!* The words become a mantra in my mind, driven by Maestro's command, and I canter past the boy and spin to face him, blocking the entrance with my body. But Tomás is smaller than the humanos who usually stand against Maestro, and he simply ducks his head and speeds beneath my belly.

Whinnying a sharp curse, I rear up and spin to follow the boy, letting my front hooves drop to the ground once I'm facing the right way . . .

And I leap to the side as a horrible scream rends the air.

I stare at the young boy. His body is sprawled face-down across the ground, his legs completely still. Only his head and arms twitch weakly, and he cries softly against the dirt.

"Tomás?"

"Ma . . . los . . ." the boy gurgles in the humano tongue. "Both . . . of . . ."

I whinny and nudge the boy with my snout, wanting to ease his breathing. He's lighter than I expect, and his body flops over onto its back, giving a soft, gurgling gasp as it lands. The boy's normally bright blue eyes are murky as they stare up at me, presenting the question his lips cannot.

Why?

I toss my head and step back from the dying boy, but I can't look away from his eyes. They hold me as they dull and the boy gives his last breath. Even then, I continue to stand there and watch his dead eyes, idly aware that the rest of the bright spots of power throughout the town have dulled and disappeared as well.

I'm still there when Maestro comes up beside me, running a hand along my side. *"Come, Mundomía,"* he nickers, cupping my chin and pulling my gaze from the dead boy's eyes. *"He made his choice. He stood against us, even though he knew the price."*

I let him pull me along, leading me out of town. No humanos stand in our way. No animales follow our movements. No bodies litter our path.

"Are we evil, Maestro?" The question finally escapes me as we press into the thick, moist underbrush beyond the town's edge.

"Now where would you get an idea like that, belleza?"

"Tomás—"

"Tomás?" Maestro interrupts. *"The boy? The one who stood against us?"* I nicker an affirmative, and Maestro shakes his head. *"Mundomía, have I ever failed you, in any way?"*

"No."

"Have I ever hurt you? Whipped you?"

"No, Maestro."

"Have I ever given you any reason to doubt me?"

I toss my head. *"Of course not, Maestro."*

"Then why are you letting a stranger, an enemigo of all people, poison you against me?"

I snort and toss my head again. *"That's not—"*

"But it is, belleza. If you let them convince you that what we do is evil, then soon you will wonder if I'm the right maestro for you, and—"

That, I can't stand for. I stop walking and stomp the ground hard with one of my front hooves. *"Never, Maestro! I would never!"*

Maestro turns to me, though I can barely make out his features in the dim lighting of the thick rainforest. I don't need to see him, however, to know he's evaluating me through our shared magia.

"Very well, belleza," he finally says. *"I believe you . . . but only if you drop this question of evil."*

"¡Sí, maestro!" I hurry to agree.

Maestro hums softly. *"Good."* After another pause, he adds, *"You know, you are my world, Mundomía, and I am yours. If we let others separate us, what will we be left with?"*

I toss my head and snort, assuring Maestro that I'll never leave him. And as we trudge forward through the underbrush, I shove all thoughts of questioning Maestro and what we do out of my mind.

But the thoughts refuse to stay away. I'm not quite sure when they creep back in; maybe they never fully disappeared. But no matter the how and when, they settle into my mind, heavy and unavoidable, and I must do something to address them.

As Maestro and I continue our routine over the next couple of months, I begin to make sure I'm closer to him whenever he confronts the villagers and townspeople. I begin to pay attention to words instead of just actions. And I begin to realize just how horrific our actions are.

Tomás is not the last to call Maestro malo. But that isn't the most common word spoken against him. Villagers ask him why he threatens them for things they would gladly barter. Townspeople claim he has no right to their secrets or treasures. Other Magos Animales stare at him in pain and horror when they realize their own animales have turned against them.

The last hurts me more than I would have thought possible.

But more than any of the words spoken against Maestro, I'm most horrified by the realization that I have no control. In one village, I balk at urging two hounds to attack an old hombre who has spoken against Maestro. The magia flows through me anyway, driven by Maestro.

In a town a week later, I rear to attack an hombre who stood against Maestro but falter when an adolescent girl dodges in front of him. I want to turn away—Tomás's dull eyes still haunt my mind—but pressure throughout my being forces me to drop to all fours before I'm ready to.

That incident makes me wonder if perhaps landing on Tomás's back that day was not the accident I thought it was. Did Maestro direct me to drop faster than I meant to? Was his command to keep the boy from leaving Taberna Cabita cover for a much more drastic command?

I'll never know the truth, but I am certain about one thing: I don't like not being in control of myself.

It starts with a second's hesitation in my use of the magia here, and a misdirection of an animal there. I can't be too obvious about disobeying Maestro—too much change in the magia would alert him, and I know all too well what he is capable of.

But I slowly work at the magia, stretching it and pulling it. I test Maestro's control with every village we visit and every town we swindle. I graduate from misdirecting one animal to misdirecting two. And when Maestro shows no sign of noticing, I move on to misdirecting three.

The process feels slow. There are times when I'm certain I'm making no progress, and sometimes fear holds me back from even pushing as far on one visit as I did on the last. But every time Maestro forces me past a hesitation or directs the magia through me despite my reluctance, I force myself to remember Tomás's dull eyes and renew my determination to claim control of myself.

The rainforest is full of life as I trot through the guarded gate of Laivena. I press forward quickly, keeping close to the pack animales being directed by a merchant. I stay close to the back, where the merchant won't notice me, certain the guards won't bother to ask the merchant for a count or question the presence of an unladen mare.

They'll probably just think I'm his mount. Like a horse can't have a purpose other than being ridden by an humano.

As soon as I'm past the gate, I turn away from the merchant's group and into a side alley. I quickly find an animal who knows the area well and convince it to show me the easiest route to traverse the entire town.

By nightfall, I stand at the edge of the town's largest square, certain Maestro will use it the next morning for his confrontation with the townspeople.

Very good, Mundomía, Maestro praises through the magia that connects us. *I will arrive in the morning.*

I barely sleep that night.

The town is bustling by the time Maestro arrives. I stand in an alleyway near the town council meeting hall, so I have a good view of the end of the square opposite the hall. On my back sprawls a young jaguar, its tail curling and extending slowly in idle interest. Around my hooves, several large rodents have gathered, chittering quietly among themselves.

The other alleyways are guarded similarly by the town's horses, large cats, rodents, snakes, and those criaturas mágicas who call the town their home (those who were simply visiting agreed to leave rather than become involved). The roofs of the buildings lining the square are filled with a colorful array of winged creatures and monkeys, which draw the murmuring awe of the townspeople filling the square.

Guards posted throughout the square eye the various accumulations of animales, but so far none of the hombres have attempted to disperse the criaturas under my control.

When Maestro enters the square, no humanos notice him. To the townspeople, he is just another persona. To the guards, just another citizen.

And to us animales? The thought is soft and distant from the magia that connects me to Maestro.

As Maestro strides toward stairs that lead up to the meeting hall, several horses, full-grown jaguars, and pardavians step into the entrances of the main roads that lead off the large square. *That* catches the attention of the humanos. The guards reach for their spears and wooden swords, while the rest of the townspeople begin to look around and murmur to each other.

Even Maestro hesitates, though I doubt anyone else notices as he smoothly transitions the stumble into a burst of speed.

Belleza? he asks as he hits the hall steps at a jog. *What are you doing?*

Lo siento, Maestro, I apologize, keeping the thoughts demure. *This town's larger than most of the others we've been to. I thought you might want a larger showing of your power at first. Maybe they'll recognize your authority without requiring a more . . . offensive showing?*

Maestro nods idly, but he has already reached the top of the steps and is turning to face the rest of the square. I drag a hoof across the ground as he puts his back to four guards.

Cálmate, Mundomía. You already have the animales ready to attack.

I softly agree and watch as he gathers all eyes to himself. I've realized over the last few months that Maestro is a performer, a dramatist. He enjoys the thrill of inciting a large group, only to cut them down all the more drastically with their own animales.

Indeed, this time is no different from previous ventures. Only the size of the audience has changed, and it even seems to be driving Maestro on: to larger claims, to larger exclamations, to larger confidences.

I'm so caught up in such thoughts that I nearly miss the moment when the guards behind Maestro lunge for him. Only the sudden tautness of the magia between us rouses me, and I barely manage to catch the strands of magia that reach through me for the birds and monkeys sitting above Maestro. Even then, several large, colorful loros flutter from the ledge before I manage to loop the magia back into my own being.

And then the cries touch my ears and sing through the magia, jerking my head upright despite my determination to remain detached. The first of the guards to reach Maestro is large and obviously strong, and the crack of his wooden sword against Maestro's back has sent him to his knees.

Shivers run through my body, unseating the young jaguar, who leaps to the ground and begins pacing across the alley's entrance. But I hardly notice. My attention is only for Maestro and for the pain that echoes through the magia and within his screams.

And the pleading.

As proud and authoritative as Maestro is, I never expected to hear him beg. Nor did I ever expect it to cut me so deeply.

Por favor, Mundomía! Why? Why have you cut me out? Why . . . ?

The shivers running through my body only increase with the damage done to Maestro's body and the pull of the magia between us. But I remain where I am, holding the magia to myself and keeping the other animales still, yet refusing to look away. This is as much a punishment for me as it is for Maestro. I've murdered, both with my own hooves and through other animales. I can't bring myself to find a Mago Animal and turn myself in, but I will take this pain upon myself as a lesson for what I allowed myself to be used for.

Belleza . . . Mundomía . . . my . . . world . . .

I flinch. The pain has piqued and is now fading, and I know it's only because Maestro is fading. That he can only speak the nombres he's given me now—

Crack!

I scream. The magia, which has been pulled taut between Maestro and me, snaps against my being. Awareness burns through me in a way it never has before. I can sense not only where every animal in the town stands, perches, or sprawls but also how it is made up and what other animales it might be related to.

No! No, no, no! I can't keep the magia! I can't—!

Hands on my muzzle make me jerk and toss my head, but the awareness of the magia pulls my mind back under and I lose all sense of the humanos around me. All I can sense is the animales who crowd close, worry and awe pressing against me from all sides.

'You are my world, Mundomía, and I am yours' . . . *Is this what he meant? That even if one of us dies . . .*

"Easy, easy, easy. *Cálmate, querida.* You're safe. You're safe."

The strange words are accompanied by strange magia, and I break free from the overwhelming awareness. The unfamiliar magia teases against my own, and while it can't influence me, I allow it to help me direct my magia back within myself. My magia feels larger than it should, but the strange magia helps me fold it within myself and reduce it into a single space within my being.

I'm breathing heavily by the time we're done, my sides heaving with the effort. When I can finally direct my attention outside of myself, I find a mujer cupping my chin with one hand and stroking my neck with the other.

"There you are," the mujer whispers, sliding her hand from behind my jaw back toward my shoulder. "Not so overwhelming now, is it?"

"No," I agree. *"Gracias."*

"Of course, querida. I could do no less for the one who saved my town."

I whinny nervously and try to pull my head from the mujer's grip, but she only shifts her hands.

"Easy, easy. I'm not going to hurt you, querida. I only want to help you."

"Why?" I demand. *"I've killed people. So many people. You can't imagine—"*

That strange magia brushes through me, and I start as I realize it isn't Magia Animal as I originally thought. It's Magia Mental.

"I think I can," the mujer answers softly. "But you were asleep then, a mere tool. What matters is what you did once you were aware, and this . . ." She waves one hand toward the square behind her. "What you did here—what you felt here—more than makes up for whatever part you might have played in his schemes."

"But his magia—"

"Is yours now, yours to do with as you please. You can use it for good now, if you like. Use it to help others."

"Can I lock it away?" The mujer hesitates, and I snort. *"You said I could do with it as I please. Can I lock it away?"*

"If that . . . is what you wish . . . then sí, you can lock it away."

"Can you help me?"

The mujer meets one of my eyes with a level gaze. "It won't help."

I snort and toss my head, finally breaking away from the mujer's grip. *"I don't care."*

The mujer sighs again and shakes her head. "Very well, querida. I'll help you lock your magia away." Without further ado, she presses the palms of her hands against the sides of my head and guides me in locking away the magia that has been my world for as long as I can remember.

Once we're done, the Mago Mental leads me to a place where I can find food. She leaves me then, assuring me as she does that I will never have to worry about sensing and controlling other animales ever again.

"Oh, and no Mago Animal will ever again be able to control you. That's something you earned for yourself; nothing will be able to take it away from you."

I thank the mujer as she leaves and watch as she disappears. Then I turn from the stable she led me to and wander toward the edge of town. I've already gained so much from this town; I won't take food from it as well.

But as much as I've gained, there is one thing I wish I hadn't. Because the mujer was right: locking the magia away didn't help to dispel my grief or my guilt.

THE GAELIC CHIEFTAIN

NEIL SLEVIN

I am the starlit horseman.

With the starlight's, rain my shadow's flecked,
stars that stream like trickling tears
from the eyes of a crying sky;

tears that streak the face of night
in grief for what's long lost—
what I alone have won, I who will not die.

Draped in ebony black
I stand alone against your darkness,
winds that shriek the curlew's call.

I know they howl to me of death
but to them I must not yield,
to them I will not fall.

I, who ride through time and space,
my horse's route no longer stone road
or rising hillside,

I, who all must pass and face,
to know my honor
and my pride.

Not even when this battle ends,
when daylight reigns and peacetime calls
will I rest; I will outlive the dawn.

I wait for it with sword's embrace,
my eternal wrath guarding the West.
My war rages on.

DREADED EDDIE

JIM HORLOCK

Swords were not known for magically appearing in piles of rubbish at the back of schoolhouses.

Edward had been staring at this one for a solid eighteen minutes, which was vastly preferable to concentrating on his arithmetic work. He was fairly certain the sword wasn't supposed to be there, and he couldn't imagine how it had arrived. One did not find swords just lying around. In fact, one did not really find swords anywhere anymore. People with swords may have been commonplace in his grandad's day, but now they tended to be arrested with extreme prejudice.

The rest of the arithmetic lesson passed at a crawl—Edward's abacus went untouched as his mind was consumed with thoughts of the sword. Edward didn't think much of mathematics in general. It was a relatively new invention, as far as he was aware, and seemed to be mainly about counting things that didn't really exist for no determinable reason. Despite being quite good at it, Edward couldn't see the use in it at all. How were imaginary melons going to help anyone? But his mother had insisted that he take up one of these new lessons because "that's the way the world is going" and because he needed to "become a man who goes places."

Edward had tried to point out that he regularly went places, including the market, the park, and despite his protests, the schoolhouse. All of this had fallen on selectively deaf ears.

Despite Edwards assurances to himself throughout the lesson that the sword outside was a weird trick of the light and couldn't be real, it stubbornly persisted in existing.

At lunchtime, he went to look at it.

He considered the sword for a good long while, ignoring the damp and unpleasant smells of the rubbish. Edward had never been particularly interested in the stories his grandad told of barbarian heroes and brave warriors who rescued princesses and fought dragons and the like. He had heard there were still savage peoples north of the Republic's borders, who wore furs and fought with axes, and there were still ogres and goblins hiding in the Wildlands. The time of the sword-wielding hero had passed, however, and the world had grown up, put on a tie, and become far less about death-defying feats of bravery and much more about tax returns and business legislation.

There didn't seem to be much room for heroics of any kind in Edward's life. It was too full of imaginary melons.

The sword in the skip did not look like a sword from one of his grandad's stories. There were no jewels in the hilt, no glowing runes along the blade, and no spiky bits. It did, however, look very sharp and quite capable of killing people. The blade was longer than his arm and glinted dully, like the eyes of a murderer.

Before Edward knew what he was doing, he had climbed among the rubbish and pulled out the sword. It was surprisingly light in his hands, and he gave it a swing.

"Ye swing like a girl," said a voice.

Edward yelped in surprise and lowered the sword, looking about sheepishly, ashamed to have been caught doing something so silly and probably dangerous. There was no one there.

"Hmm, let's see," the voice continued. *"A bit young. On the weak side, too. So was I when I started, though. I reckon I can work with ye."*

"Um . . ." said Edward. "Who's there?"

"Where are you?" he added a moment later, because he'd have felt more comfortable about the situation if he at least knew where the voice was coming from.

"Not too bright, though, are ye? Still, I suppose ye don't have to be . . . My old mate Na'an the Barbarian was thick as a pig, but a hell of a scrapper."

"What's going on?" Edward asked with increasing concern. The sword had been weird enough, but a disembodied voice was more strangeness than he was prepared to deal with in a single afternoon.

"What did ye think would happen if ye picked up a magic sword, laddie?"

Edward looked down at the sword doubtfully.

"It doesn't look very magic," he said.

"The magic ones never do," the voice replied sagely.

"Look, is this some kind of joke?" asked Edward, doubting more and more each second that it was. There was no one to look at, so he addressed the sword directly.

"Not at all, laddie," said the voice. *"Ain't ever been more serious. I've been waitin' for the chosen one. Ye must be the chosen one cos ye picked up the sword, see? Stands to reason."*

"Chosen one?" asked Edward, not sure he was liking the sound of this. "Chosen for what?"

"To save the world, lad," said the voice. *"What else are chosen ones chosen for? Are ye that dense?"*

Edward decided he was starting to dislike this voice. He wondered if all swords were this rude.

"Who are you?" he demanded. "Tell me where you are."

"I'm in ya head, lad," said the voice. *"And in the sword. Mostly in the sword. It's a magic sword, ye see?"*

Edward got the feeling that the voice didn't exactly know the answer to the question either. He tried to throw the sword down and leap away. He succeeded with the leaping bit, but not the "away" or the "throwing down" since he couldn't release his grip on the handle.

"Now, now, laddie," said the voice. *"No need to panic. I've been waitin' a long time for the chosen one. Can't have ye droppin' the sword and runnin', now can I?"*

"Please let me go," pleaded Edward, fear and panic rising in his gut like a bad dinner seeking revenge.

"Don't be afraid, lad," said the voice. *"We've just got a little quest to go on, that's all."*

Edward didn't want to go on a quest, no matter what the size.

"Um . . ." he said by way of protest.

"That's not my name, lad," said the voice. *"Though I did know a barbarian called Um once. Big bloke. Could eat a whole duck without chewin'. Think he joined a sect of mad monks in the end."*

"I have a geography lesson," said Edward lamely. "I'll miss it if I go with you."

"Ye're welcome," said the voice.

"Look, I wouldn't even know how to start a quest!" Edward protested.

"That's easy, lad. We go to the pub."

The only pub Edward knew was the Bells and Trumpet, at the corner of the market in town, and he only knew about that because the positioning of the eponymous instruments on the sign was vaguely rude and therefore amusing to people too young to drink there.

As he made his way there, he was very aware of the sword at his belt and so was everyone else. People gave him a wide berth on the street, determinedly looking away from him in a way that suggested they were actually looking at him very closely. Edward was certain several of them were rushing off to fetch the City Guard as soon as he had passed.

"What's the matter with these people?" the voice asked. *"Haven't they ever seen a sword before?"*

"Actually, they probably haven't," said Edward. "Except maybe in a museum. Swords are banned in the city."

"What about the guards?"

"They're armed with truncheons. Hard bits of wood."

"Clubs? What good is that if a dragon or an army of trolls shows up?"

"Um," said Edward awkwardly. "You're not really allowed to call them that anymore. Well, I mean, they can call each other the T word ,but we're supposed to call them rock-kin. And dragons have been extinct for about a hundred years."

The sword went quiet but Edward got the distinct impression it was looking around. How exactly a sword could do that, he had no idea.

"This was all different when I was alive, ye know," said the voice. It sounded almost remorseful. *"Everyone looks so clean. Can't trust a clean person. And these houses were much more flammable. How's someone supposed to keep up if people keep changin' things all the time? Why can't we just stick to the good old ways?"*

Edward stayed tactfully quiet. If his history lessons were anything to go by, the old ways had mostly involved plague, famine, and war, none of which sounded particularly appealing.

"Hang on," he said. "What do you mean, 'when you were alive'?"

"Never mind that," huffed the voice, apparently still grumpy about the clean streets, healthy people, and lack of dragons. *"How far away is this pub, anyway?"*

"Not far now. Look, I'm not really allowed in there without an adult."

"What? Why not?"

"Well, I'm not old enough to drink."

"Can't drink? What do ye do when ye're thirsty?"

"I mean I can't drink alcohol."

"Why in the Seven Hells not? Is it a religious thing? I once knew a sect of monks that wouldn't drink. No wonder they were mad as loons. Worshipped a giant pineapple."

"What? No, it's not a religious thing, it's just the law. I can't go in without an adult."

"I'm an adult."

"You're a sword."

"A sword will get ye in more places than an adult, laddie."

Edward looked down at the sword. It had allowed him to release his grip on the handle once he'd sheathed it. Perhaps, if he was quick enough, he could just undo his belt and throw it away with the sword attached . . .

"Don't even think about it, laddie," warned the voice. "I'm not just in the sword, remember?"

Edward felt his hand twitch and knew it was no random spasm; it was a warning.

Edward hadn't been sure what to expect from the bar apart from not being allowed in.

The people inside, however, paid him no mind as he entered. He was pleasantly surprised by the interior. It was a high-ceilinged, open place, well-lit by large windows and spacious despite many large round tables. A few families were in attendance, eating their meals and trying to keep their children under control with varying degrees of success. An elderly gent sat alone at the bar, reading a paper.

"What kind of bar is this, laddie?"

"The only one I know of. It seems nice to me."

"The floor isn't crunchy."

"Is it supposed to be?"

"Aye. That's what happens after years of broken glass and crumbled teeth. And where's the dartboard full of knives? And the gang of surly cardplayers?"

"I don't think it has any of that stuff," said Edward, feeling glad it didn't.

"Well, it'll have to do. A bar is a bar, right enough, although ye shouldn't trust one without a crunchy floor—remember that. Sit in a corner."

Edward started to move.

"Not that one! A dark one!"

Finding a dark corner proved a challenge in the bright and airy pub, but he picked the dimmest one he could find and the voice made no protest. Edward sat down and wondered vaguely how long it would be before the City Guard turned up to arrest him.

"Now what?" he asked in a whisper so he wouldn't be overheard talking to a sword.

"Eh?" came the reply. *"Speak up, lad! I'm not as young as I used to be!"*

Edward strongly suspected the sword was just playing it up at this point. It had read his thoughts earlier, and he didn't think deafness was a common problem for things made of steel. He wasn't brave enough to call the sword on it, though, so instead he settled for raising his voice to a low mumble and repeating the question.

"Now we wait," said the voice. So Edward waited.

"What are we waiting for?" he asked after a few moments.

"For a fight to break out," said the voice, as though this was the most obvious thing in the world.

Edward looked around. A pair of brothers, part of a small family near the door, looked as though they might start to squabble. They were about ten years old. The elderly man by the bar coughed.

"I don't think anyone's going to start a fight."

"Trust me. There's always a bar fight. Part of the quest, see?"

A few minutes passed. The only sign of the prophesied conflict was when the young brothers did indeed begin to bicker. Edward didn't think that counted.

"What's that?" asked the voice, and Edward experienced the peculiar sensation of something inside him pointing.

"It's a menu."

"What's it for?" asked the voice suspiciously.

"You use it to order food and drinks," explained Edward.

The voice seemed to consider this for a moment.

"Well, tell it I want some grog."

"What's grog?"

"You know! Grog! Mead! Ale! Booze! Beer! Drink!"

"All right, all right," said Edward. "But can you even drink? I mean, you're a voice in a sword. What do you want me to do? Pour it in your sheath and dunk you?"

"There's no need for cheek, lad," growled the voice.

"Cheek?" Edward's temper flared. "You're basically holding me hostage! You've made me miss school, so I'll probably get expelled! And because I'm forced to carry you around, I'll probably get arrested! They'll throw me in the city dungeon, and then my mother will come, and she will actually kill me!"

Edward realized his voice had risen to a shout. He was breathing hard, practically panting, and his hands had curled into fists on the wooden tabletop. The staff and other patrons were very pointedly not noticing him. One of the barmaids was not noticing him so hard that the pint she was pouring had overflowed and she hadn't realized.

"That's the spirit, lad!" said the voice. *"Have a little fire! Now, what do ye want to know?"*

"Why are we really here?" he asked quietly, trying to ignore the fact he was now blushing furiously.

"Eh? Speak up!"

"You don't even have ears!" Edward whispered furiously, finding the courage after all.

"All right, all right," said the voice. *"Calm down. I told ye, we're here for the fight. There's always a bar fight at the start of an epic quest."*

"And I told you," said Edward, getting angry again, "I don't think anyone's going to start a—"

The doors slammed open, and half a dozen armored men marched in. The truncheons at their belts and the badges embossed on their breastplates marked them as members of the City Guard. Edward paled.

It took them no time at all to spot Edward in his not-dark-at-all corner.

"You!" said their leader, a captain judging by the plumage on his helm. "Don't move! You're under arrest for possession of a deadly weapon and the public bearing of arms! Disarm yourself slowly! Do *not* resist!"

Edward tried to raise his hands meekly but found they were locked in place on the table.

"There are seven of them," he whispered frantically to the sword.

"Never mind how many there are, lad. Ye've got to stand up for the little guy. That's a hero's job!"

"What little guy?"

"Ye seem little enough to me, lad."

The guards fanned out in front of his table, cutting off all routes of escape. Their hands were on the handles of their truncheons.

"Give 'em The Look."

"What?" whispered Edward.

"The Look!" urged the voice as the captain repeated his speech about not resisting.

"I have no idea what you're talking about!" said Edward.

"I'm not saying it again, kid," said the captain. "Come along quietly now. Last chance."

Edward felt someone else's grin break out across his face and a wild glint appear in his eyes.

"I don't think so."

"Don't worry yaself about it," said the voice cheerfully.

Edward looked around his cell gloomily. They had remodeled the dungeons in recent years to keep up with new laws regarding humane treatment of prisoners. The cell was spacious and well lit, with none of the damp or the rats he'd been expecting. Still, he was in a pretty bad mood. His face throbbed painfully, and he avoided touching it. He was pretty sure his nose was broken.

"Ye didn't do that badly," consoled the voice. *"Ye're only young, and this is ya first time heroizin'. Lots still to learn. Besides, ye've got to end up in a dungeon at some point on the quest, or ye're doin' it wrong."*

Somehow, Edward did not feel comforted. They had probably contacted his mother already. No number of magic swords would save him from her wrath.

He looked down at the weapon. No matter how the guards had tried, they'd been unable to remove it from his person. Eventually, they'd just given up but somewhat lamely made him promise not to draw it.

"Remember when ye smashed the bottle on that bloke's head?" the voice continued. *"That was pretty good! Ingenuity, that was!"*

Edward looked at his bandaged hand. A deep red throb still emanated from the palm, where the glass had splintered.

"When you did, you mean?" he asked grumpily.

"Nay, lad. That was ya own doin'. I wouldn've tried. Tricky things, bottles."

Edward frowned and thought back. He remembered grabbing the bottle from the bar. He remembered swinging it. Had it really been him? He'd been terrified throughout the fight, from the start to finish. His heart had never pounded so hard. There had been lightning in his veins. He'd felt alive, so much more alive than when he sat in a classroom working at his studies.

"Is this what being a hero is like?"

"Aye, lad," said the voice wistfully. *"Tis a glorious life. Wanderin' the land and sleepin' under the stars. Bar fights and darin' escapes from the deepest dungeons. Navigatin' mazes of death-traps to recover lost treasure from ancient temples. Fightin' dragons and witches and monsters of all kinds."*

"And protecting the innocent?" Edward ventured. The list of heroic exploits had not inspired him. So far, it seemed to him like being a hero was mostly homelessness, followed by imprisonment, with the occasional theft and drunken brawl along the way.

"Oh, aye!" agreed the voice. *"Damsels in distress, poor villagers under the threat of evil tyrants, even the odd king."*

That was more like it. Edward liked the sound of helping people.

"How do you help them?"

"Usually by killin' the thing that's causin' the problems."

"Oh. Does that make the villagers less poor?"

"I'm a hero, lad, not a moneylender."

"What about the damsels? What happens after you rescue them?"

"How should I know? The rescuin' bit is my job. Once that's done, I leave 'em to it."

"What, in the middle of nowhere?"

The sword sniffed. *"I'll give 'em a lift to the nearest village if I've got a horse at the time."*

Edward frowned some more. He was getting good at it. This whole hero business seemed pretty irresponsible to him. What good was rescuing a damsel if you left her to wander the woods alone afterward and get eaten by wolves? What good was getting rid of a tyrant if the villagers were just as poor afterward?

"What we need to do," said the sword, *"is give you a proper hero name."*

"A name?"

"Aye, all the greats had names. Na'an the Barbarian. Arogath the Destroyer. Rurugan the Sunderer. Red Carl."

"Red Carl?"

"Oh, aye. He defeated an entire sect of mad flesh-eating monks with only a broken sword and a rusty codpiece."

"What is it with you and sects of monks?" asked Edward, wondering what a codpiece was.

The voice inside him shrugged. It was a strange feeling.

"Monks are always trouble. Well-known fact. Anyway, back to the namin'. Very important, a hero name. Strikes fear into the hearts of your enemies. Inspires hope in the people. Very important that, inspirin' hope. Part of the hero's job. Integral, ye might say. How do ye feel about Edward the Great?"

"I don't feel particularly great . . ."

"How about Edward the Bloody? Edward Head-Taker? Dreaded Eddie?"

"What was your hero name? Who are you?"

"Tell ye what, lad. I reckon ye've earned it. I'll show ye who I am."

Edward felt as though his head were being forced open by a crowbar made of lightning. The cell around him fell away, and he was wrapped in sudden darkness. The sensation lasted less than a second but left an echo of agony reverberating in his mind.

When he pulled himself together, he found himself looking through someone else's eyes.

It was a peculiar sensation, like looking out at the world through a pair of small tunnels. It took Edward a good few moments to come to grips with it and stop feeling dizzy and sick.

As far as Edward could tell, the eyes in question belonged to a young boy. He was short, judging by the nearby trees, and his hands were small, pink, and unmarred, coming into Edward's view as they pumped at the air. The boy was running. Edward realized he was party to the boy's other senses, too. Smoke stung his nostrils, and somewhere close behind him, the screams of men and horses cut ragged through the dawn air. A battle.

The boy was being chased. He could hear heavy breathing and charging footsteps. Not just running, then, but running for his life.

Suddenly, he tripped and fell, treating Edward to a whirling view of ground-then-sky-then-ground several times in rapid succession as the boy went tumbling down a hill. As the boy pulled himself back to his feet, body ringing with pain, his eyes came to rest on the sword.

It wasn't pretty. It didn't have gold or jewels. There were no glowing runes or spiky bits. As the boy was drawn to touch the hilt, Edward knew what was going to happen. By the time the raiders reached the boy, it was too late for them—he'd drawn the sword. They didn't stand a chance.

When the slaughter was done, the boy found he couldn't drop the sword. And that was the beginning of it.

The years rolled by as Edward watched, and the boy became a young man. The sword bullied and chided and pushed the boy from fear and weakness into courage and strength. He was always underestimated, always outnumbered, but always victorious in the end. On his quest for revenge against those who burned his village, he fought monsters and bandits and foiled death again and again. It was every origin of a hero that Edward had ever heard.

"Your village was burned down," he said. "Then you found a magic sword and set out on a quest for vengeance? Isn't that a bit cliché?"

"Nothing wrong with a cliché," said the voice huffily. *"My ma used to make a lovely cliché."*

After a moment's consideration, Edward said, "I think you mean quiche."

"I know what I meant! Respect ya elders!"

"Right. Sorry."

Edward returned his attention to the story unfolding before him. The man had become a hero of legend. Slaying dragons and vanquishing demons had become second nature to him, almost a reflex. He had changed a lot, but the world was changing too. People weren't so happy when he burned down a barn to kill the ghoul inside. The villagers turned on him when he killed their count for being a vampire. More and more damsels rescued themselves, more and more people greeted him with wariness and even fear, as though he were a violent criminal, not a figure to be admired and celebrated.

Finally, the hero grew old and haggard, but this was a man for whom defiance was now a default response. He had refused to bow to kings and submit to gods; why would the changing of the world phase him?

It was then he had the idea. It was then he sought out the sorcerer.

"You had yourself put into a sword?" asked Edward as realization dawned.

"Aye, lad. My body was starting to slow down by then, but that didn't have to be the end. As I was trained, so I would train another. A chosen one. Someone who could put the world right."

"Put the world right?" Edward rather thought people should be free not to have their property destroyed and their leaders murdered. "How?"

"By the Gods, ye're slow! That's the quest we're on, laddie! We're saving the world!"

"Okay, I've seen enough," said Edward. "You can stop this."

What happened next was strange, which Edward pretty much expected today—strange seemed to be the only dish on the menu. It was as though his eyes were being forced to look in two directions at once. One was still in the past, where the hero was making some heavily armed guards seriously regret their life decisions. In the other, Edward could see his arms moving in time with the hero in the past, sword swinging in perfect unison.

Then, with a kind of mental twang, the past disappeared entirely, and Edward was left looking out of his own eyes. They were not where he had left them.

"You broke us out of the dungeon? How?" he cried, aghast at the carnage in the corridor.

"Ah, one of the usual ways I'm sure. Hooking the keys off a big loop on the

guard's belt is a favorite. Or charming the beautiful general of the evil king with ya rugged looks so she'll come to free ye and betray her master. Or training ya pet monkey, bird, dog, or whatever to fetch ye the keys. Not for me, that one. Never was any good with animals."

"But you don't remember which of those you did? None of them seem to suit this situation."

"When ye've done these things as many times as me, lad, they all merge into one. Every dungeon is the same when ye get right down to it. Falls under 'facin' impossible odds.'"

"What do you mean?"

"Well, would ye say breakin' out of that dungeon was impossible?"

"I suppose so . . ."

"Then it's a hero's work. Stands to reason, that does. If I had a penny for every time I'd done something someone said was impossible . . ." The voice paused for a moment, trying to work out how to spend its imaginary riches. *"I'd have had myself put in a better class of sword. Maybe some nice jewels about the hilt or a skull on the sheath. Somethin' classy. Anyway, the point is: facin' impossible odds, lad. It's in the job description."*

The sword piloted his body onward, stepping over the fallen guards.

"Where are we going?" Edward asked, dreading the answer.

"The emperor's throne room."

"We don't really have an emperor. This is a republic. We have a minister primus and a council to support him."

"We'll go to his throne room, then."

"He doesn't have a throne room. I think he has an office. I saw a picture of it in the paper from when he signed a bill to grant religious freedoms to witches."

"See? That's exactly the kind of thing we're goin' to put a stop to. It's not right, bein' an evil tyrant and not havin' a proper throne room. And this fortress is a disgrace. No lava pits. No piles of skulls. No spiky things on the walls. What's that?"

"A potted plant."

"Does it shoot poison darts?"

"I doubt it. I think it might be plastic, actually."

The voice grumbled.

"Right," it said, deciding to ignore the apparently offensive decor. *"When we get there, ye've got to look the part, all right? Just walk up and kick the door in, then give The Look."*

"I'm not sure I want to do that . . ."

"Trust me, laddie, we need to make an impression."

The doors were made of rich, dark wood with a pair of stylish bronze handles, which the voice completely ignored as it used Edward's foot to kick them open.

They swung inward with a mighty boom and revealed a large office with thick carpet, several waiting chairs, and a rather imposing desk set before a huge window. A secretary looked up at them from behind the desk, night-black eyes narrowing dangerously over the rims of her gold-rimmed glasses.

"This is the place," said Edward. It was something of a relief to find it after all the other doors they'd kicked in. The gentleman in the bathroom had been most upset.

"Right." The voice marched them right up to the desk and brought the sword down in an overhead chop, sundering the wood almost in two. The secretary barely moved, instead fixing Edward with a glare that could probably have been used to burn small villages to the ground.

"What," she said, brandishing the 'h' in 'what' like a weapon, "is the meaning of this?"

"Tell her ye demand to see the emperor!"

"I keep telling you, there is no emperor!" hissed Edward.

"Ye know what I mean!"

"I'm waiting," said the secretary, whose tone could have been used to cut diamonds.

"Um . . ." said Edward, which he was aware probably wasn't a good start. "I'm here to see the minister primus."

The gaze of the secretary became no less intense in the silence that followed. Edward thought he even felt the voice faltering.

"Do you have an appointment?" she asked in a tone that suggested she already knew the answer and just needed him to admit it so she could legally disembowel him.

"Show her ye're serious! Give her The Look!"

"I keep telling you, I don't know how!"

"If you don't have an appointment, then you can't see the minister primus. Make an appointment at the Appointments Office."

The secretary was apparently unfazed by hearing half a conversation a stranger wielding a sword was having with himself.

"Maybe ravish her a bit?"

"I will not!" protested Edward hotly.

Slowly and with the terrible inevitability of an approaching tidal wave, the secretary stood. Edward felt himself take a step back and wasn't sure whether it was he or the voice that had moved his legs.

"Well!" she began.

"It's all right, Miriam," said a voice from behind them.

The minister primus had entered through a side door that evidently led to his office. He wasn't overly tall or handsome. His clothes were expensive, but not extravagant, and about his brow was a plain silver circlet—a symbol of his office. The voice practically growled at the sight of him.

"Why don't you take an early lunch?" he said. "I will handle this myself."

"Of course, sir," said Miriam, the Secretary of Doom, whose demeanor had changed from archdemoness to delightful upon the arrival of the minister primus. She stepped around her shattered desk and left the room as though nothing unusual had happened.

"Now what?" Edward whispered from the corner of his mouth.

"Now, we kill the bastard!"

"Kill him? I don't want to kill him! You didn't say anything about killing him!"

"It's people like him that've destroyed everything! They've ruined the world! He's an evil sorcerer! He'll turn into a giant snake in a minute, mark my words!"

"I certainly will not," said the primus.

"You can hear him?" asked Edward, stunned.

"Oh, yes, of course," the primus replied casually. He leaned in the doorway and regarded Edward as though he were no more a threat than a goldfish.

"Because he's a sorcerer!" cried the voice in the sword. *"I knew it! He's got everyone here under his spell! I knew it wasn't right, guards not carrying swords and dungeons not having rats and all the rest of it!"*

"He is not a sorcerer!" said Edward.

"I am, actually," said the primus, inspecting his fingernails briefly.

Edward stared at him, mouth open.

"What?" he managed after several unsuccessful vowel sounds.

"I am a sorcerer. Possibly the most powerful still alive, in fact."

"Told you!"

"Shut up! Is everyone here under your spell?"

"Gods, no. I never could stand all that mind-control stuff. Exhausting. Far easier to inspire loyalty simply by being a good employer. My staff get excellent benefits—annual holidays, full pension, and medical care."

"I don't know what he just said, but it sounds like an incantation to me! Get ready, lad!"

"Edward Henry Ford," said the primus, stunning Edward through the use of his full name.

"You . . . you know me?" he managed.

"Since this morning, yes. When a young boy picks up a magic sword in my city, I like to be kept informed of the situation. And who do you have inside there, I wonder?"

"It doesn't matter what my name is. I'm the last hero! And I'm going to put things back the way they were!"

"Really? You think killing me will bring the dragons back from extinction? Undo technological and philosophical advancement? Unwrite laws that create more freedom and more education for the people? I rather think not."

Edward's arms raised the sword.

"I'd advise against that," said the primus, raising a hand, not in threat as much as caution. "Killing me really wouldn't make a difference, even if you were capable of doing it. I also feel I should point out that creating change in the world, no matter how much you may dislike it, doesn't make me an evil man."

The primus narrowed his eyes.

"And you know that, don't you? Hmm . . . so what's your game? A death wish, perhaps? You want to 'go down fighting'? No, that doesn't seem right either . . ."

"Get ready, lad!" said the voice. *"Remember what I taught you about a hero's job. Remember that there should always be heroes!"*

"Wait!" Edward cried, but his body was already leaping.

Edward saw it in slow motion as he sailed through the air. He felt his arm draw back the sword. He saw the primus raise a hand, a look of genuine remorse on his face. He saw the lightning crackle from the primus's palm.

The world briefly flashed white, and Edward was on his back. For a second or two, the ceiling of the office spun overhead and he forgot where he was.

"Are you all right?"

Edward pulled himself upright and looked down at his hand. There was a sword hilt there, but the blade was gone, broken and melted. Memory sprang on him in a saber-toothed ambush.

"No!" he cried, looking at the scattered shards of metal on the floor. He scrambled to pick them up, thinking that perhaps if he could piece them back together somehow . . . but they were too hot, and he dropped them straightaway with a hiss of pain.

"You killed him," he said, looking up at the primus. It was not an accusation, merely a statement of fact.

"I'm afraid so," the primus replied, his face severe. "He rather left me no choice, I'm afraid. I had to choose between hitting the sword and hitting you. The latter would have killed you. He knew what I would do."

"You think he wanted to die?" asked Edward. He felt numb. He had wanted nothing more than to get rid of the sword since he picked it up, but now that it was broken and the voice inside him was unmistakably absent, he suddenly felt empty.

"I think this was his last adventure," said the primus. "He knew this wasn't his world anymore—that his time had passed. But he had things to pass on before he was ready to give up. Do you remember his last words?"

"There must always be heroes," Edward repeated, staring down at the broken blade.

"Indeed. This quest of his was never about me. It was about you. You were his chosen one."

"What does that mean?" asked Edward. He just wanted to go home, curl up in bed, and close his eyes, hoping that when he opened them again this would all have been an improbable dream.

"The world still needs heroes, Edward. Just not his kind of hero. People still need rescuing; they still need someone to stand up for them, to be an inspiration, a figure of hope. But the evils of the world today aren't things you can kill with a sword. He knew that, or he'd have gone and killed them himself. Today's problems are greed, famine, ignorance, poverty, and hatred. You need a different kind of hero for those kinds of things."

"You think that's what he wanted me to do?" Edward suddenly felt very small. Sticking a sword into a dragon and surviving was one thing, but how did you beat something like ignorance?

"I'm sure of it," said the primus. "He needed someone born into this world, someone who understood it. I have begun the work myself, of course. Free education for all, religious freedoms for all, rights for minority groups . . . but there is so much to be done, Edward, and I am an elected official with a limited term of office. When my time is up, there are many who, upon taking my place, will begin to undo my good works."

"Are you saying you want me to replace you?" The blood in Edward's brain seemed to be going about its business at a much louder volume than was usual.

"Not just yet, my boy," chuckled the primus. "I have a few years still, and you have much to learn, but I will be watching your progress with interest."

He put a hand on Edward's shoulder and began to guide him toward the exit. Edward looked down at his hands. He was still holding the handle of the shattered sword.

"Keep it," the primus suggested, following his gaze. "A reminder of what a hero can be and what a hero should be."

Edward frowned. What was a hero? Just a thug who went around stabbing monsters and stealing from monks? If that was all they were, why did people look up to them so? Why were their stories still told? Perhaps it was more about what they represented. What was it the voice had said about the job of a hero? Facing impossible odds, inspiring hope in the people, standing up for the little guy (even if that guy was you), and never trusting a bar that didn't have the requisite levels of crunchiness underfoot?

Dreaded Eddie looked down at the sword hilt and saw possibility.

PR

ADAM CARLSON

Jim pulled up in front of the ramshackle restaurant in his best suit. It was not a particularly expensive suit, but it was the best Jim could afford, dark and professional. First impressions were important; customers needed to know that they were talking to a serious businessman. He picked a folder up off the front seat and stepped out of the car.

The area was quiet. All the emergency vehicles, with their sirens and flashing lights, had left hours earlier. A man—probably the owner—sat on the curb in front of the establishment, trying to ignore the havoc that had been wrought.

Jim approached cautiously, unsure how to proceed. Usually, he liked to sneak around among the rubberneckers and see the damage firsthand, but today had been busy and he'd missed the crowd. If he walked past the owner to look at the scene, he might appear apathetic about the people involved, and that was an image his employer couldn't afford. Besides, with the gaping hole in the wall, what else did Jim really need to know?

"Excuse me." Jim waited for a reaction—a flick of the eyes, a slightly raised chin—but there was nothing. Jim cleared his throat and raised his voice. "May I sit here?" This time, Jim took the silence as acceptance and sat down.

The restaurateur appeared to be in his late forties with a bit of a paunch and a hairline that had chosen to recede rather than give in to the gray that crept in around his ears. His hands twiddled with a towel.

"Tough day, huh?"

The owner gave a half-sigh, half-sob.

"Sorry, I guess that's sort of inadequate. This must be terrible."

"You don't know the half of it," the owner croaked.

"I'm sure I don't," Jim admitted. "I see this kind of thing all the time, and I have to admit that I don't understand how people can deal with it."

The owner gave him a sideways glance and pointed a thumb over his shoulder at the building. "You see this a lot?"

"More than I'd like to." He stuck out his hand. "I'm Jim."

The owner looked at the hand skeptically but didn't take it. "Roberto."

Jim dropped his hand, taking the awkward refusal in stride. "On behalf of my employer, I would like to apologize that this event took place on your property."

"Employer?"

Jim swallowed and cleared his throat. This was where he'd have to dig in and start the real sales pitch. "I work for the Crimson Crusader." Even after months on the job, Jim had to fight the urge to cringe at the pseudonym. What kind of moron would choose such a tacky nom de plume for his superhero name? Jim's first suggestion as the public representative was to change the name, but the Crusader wouldn't budge.

Roberto turned fully to Jim, eyes widening. "You work for him?"

"Yes, I—"

The owner stood, quivering with rage. "That red bastard did this!"

Jim held up his hands. "Whoa! I'm here to help."

"You want to help? You tell that super asshole to stay away from my restaurant!"

Jim blinked. "Well, I suppose . . . I *could* do that. But . . . no, never mind. You probably wouldn't be interested."

Roberto relaxed a little but maintained an air of cynicism. "Interested in what?"

"Forget I mentioned it." Jim always felt bad when he had to bait victims like this, but he rationalized that it was okay because he was working for a good guy. Asinine moniker notwithstanding, the Crimson Crusader was a superhero.

"You think you can fix everything?"

"Hey, I didn't say that. Sure, the Crusader is super strong and fast, but there are limitations to what he can do. I doubt that you would want to wait for him to have time to fix the whole building."

"I didn't think so."

"But that doesn't mean that we'll sit idly by while you have to rebuild all by yourself." Jim walked toward the decrepit building, hands up, trying to paint a scene with his words. "Picture this: We have tacos for donations. People can get their pictures taken with the Crusader for a fee. We have a foot race—entry is five dollars and the winner gets to run with CC. Hell, we can tear down the rest of the wall and sell pieces, like they did in Berlin."

He was close enough that he patted the wall, and another brick gave up its tentative grip to crash loudly among the rubble. Jim ignored it and went on. "The mayor will be here, maybe even the governor. You'll get your picture in the paper, and we'll raise enough money to hire local contractors to fix up the restaurant, make it better than it was. And the Crimson Crusader will be the first person in line when you reopen. Not only will it cover the costs, it'll make you a celebrity. People will come in droves to eat your Mexican food. What do you think?"

The owner didn't look up from the hand towel he was twisting in his hands. "You think that will fix everything?"

Jim opened his mouth but didn't know how to respond. Really, the answer was "No," but he couldn't tell that to the man he was trying to negotiate with. *Swindle*, Jim thought. *That's what you're trying to do. If you were negotiating, you would be honest instead of omitting important facts.*

Although superheroes had just come to the foreground of culture in the last couple of years, insurance companies had learned quickly to avoid paying for damages that resulted from superhero battles since such incidents were not specifically covered in the contracts. Several lawsuits were slowly making their way to the Supreme Court, but it would still be years before anyone saw any money, if they ever did.

Many superheroes had begun hosting fundraisers for people who had been injured and businesses that were damaged during battles. Unfortunately, they had largely run their course, and the returns had been diminishing for months. The first time you get your picture taken with a superhero, it's worth the charge of admission. After a dozen such events, who really needs it? The supply was too high to expect yet another fundraiser to provide the money to repair the restaurant.

That meant that the old man might have to sue to try to get the money to repair his restaurant, but villains wouldn't pay and heroes generally didn't have money. Hell, Jim was only working for the Crimson Crusader for peanuts so he could earn the experience to get a good job later. The whole issue was becoming more convoluted and intriguing with the addition of an argument on behalf of superheroes that any destruction resulting from a superhero battle was an act of God; therefore, they could not be responsible. Although that lawsuit was still being decided, the ramifications would be widespread, and the argument had gotten religious protesters involved who claimed that superheroes weren't gods. Atheists tended to be split. Some argued that there were no gods while others argued that if superheroes could be sued then the church could be sued as a representative of God.

Jim omitted all that information, but he felt it was okay because he really was trying to help the poor man whose restaurant had practically been demolished. If they didn't have the fundraiser, then there was no way the business would be able to reopen. Jim had the owner's best interest at heart, no matter how underhanded his methods were.

He turned and looked into the restaurant, where shattered tables and chairs were strewn about. In the shadows at the back of the building, he saw it.

"Is that a car?"

"Your boss threw it through the front door!"

"I'm sorry, I just . . . I didn't realize."

"I ought to sue him for everything he's worth."

"Let's not be too hasty." Jim pulled a sheet of paper out of the manila folder. Ideally, he'd rather present it while the victim was excited about the prospect of a fundraiser. But he couldn't let this conversation get further out of hand. "I want you to look at this document for a minute."

"What is it?"

"Just take a look and see what you think."

Jim handed it over and waited for any questions.

Roberto waved the paper when he'd finished reading it. "You want me to sign this?"

Jim pulled out a pen. "If you'd be willing."

"It's a lie."

"Oh, it's just . . . all it says is that the Crimson Crusader was not responsible for the damages." Whether or not the paper was legally binding was questionable, but having the owner sign it would definitely make it more difficult for him to file a lawsuit later. "It explains that you, as a witness, hold the instigator of the fight . . . um, who was CC fighting?"

"The Jackal."

Now there was a real supervillain name. Hell, the Jackal didn't even really have special powers, just a metal jaw that gave him a strong bite, but his name inspired fear and gave u a sense of who he was. Jim was sure that the Jackal must have a brilliant PR guy.

"All the paper says is that the Jackal is responsible. I'm sure that CC would be willing to capture him and help in any lawsuit you choose to file."

"It's a lie!" Roberto crumpled the paper and threw it down.

"What do you mean?"

"That red bastard started it!"

Jim looked blank. "That's not possible. He doesn't start fights."

"He started this one. My customers were just waiting for food when he tossed a Chevy through the wall."

"But you said the Jackal was here."

"He ordered a burrito."

"The Jackal? The evil mastermind? He just . . . ordered food?"

"And waited patiently."

This was ridiculous. Who would believe that a supervillain was sitting around, ordering food, when a superhero began rampaging and destroyed a local business? "The Crimson Crusader is a hero."

"Not today, he's not."

Jim knelt and picked up the crumpled paper, smoothing it out as best he could. If the Crusader had done it, then it made everything Jim was doing even worse. Ensuring that a guilty villain received all the blame and helping raise money for repairs, even if it wouldn't be enough, was at least trying to help. If blaming the Jackal was an outright lie, that made the Crusader a villain, didn't it? In disbelief, Jim repeated the only truth he could imagine. "The Jackal started it."

"You think I lie?"

"No, you just . . . he did something that you didn't even notice, and then CC retaliated."

"You think I'm stupid?"

"No, of course I don't. Just give me one minute." Jim turned away, pulled out his phone, and dialed his employer, unsure if he really wanted the scarlet buffoon to answer or not.

"Hi," CC's voice drawled with overconfidence and ineptitude. "You're lucky I answered. I just bagged the Jackal and tossed him into jail."

All of Jim's worry vanished in momentary exhilaration. "You caught the Jackal?"

"Sometimes, it's almost too easy."

"That's amazing." It really was. In over three months of working for the Crusader, Jim had never known him to actually capture a criminal. "What . . . uh, what did he do?"

"Do?"

"Yeah, what charges will he be brought up on? I'm at the Mexican restaurant . . ."

"You're taking care of that? Good man."

"Yeah, but the owner doesn't want to sign the agreement. He says the Jackal was just . . . eating. What was he really doing?"

"Uh . . ."

"Was he robbing the place? Did he brainwash everyone? Is that why the owner doesn't remember?"

"That's a good one. We can use it."

Jim felt like his insides suddenly turned to ice. "What do you mean?"

"Yeah, we'll say he brainwashed everyone."

Jim glanced at the owner, who looked more angry than brainwashed. "I don't understand what you're saying."

"You'll fix it. And by the way, you'll want to stop by the prison."

"Why?"

"To smooth things over. Make some publicity about fixing the hole."

"What hole?"

"Where I dropped the Jackal."

Jim's eyes widened, threatening to pop out of his head. "You literally dropped him?"

"And while you're there, tell them about the brainwashing whatsit."

"But you can't just drop him through the roof! That's not how justice works!"

"I think it worked pretty well."

"But—"

"Gotta go. You take care of those details; you're good at that. Right now, I'm on the trail of the Scorpions Tail."

Jim's mind shifted gears from belligerent disbelief to concern and intrigue. The Scorpions Tail was a small-time crook whose biggest crime was arguably the lack of apostrophe in his name. Originally, he had left a severed tail as his calling card at each scene, but he either got stung too many times or realized that paper is more difficult to track than arachnid appendages. As far as Jim knew, there had only been a few small-time robberies attributable to him since he'd gotten out from his last stint in the penitentiary.

"What is the Scorpions Tail doing?"

"I don't know, but you'll figure something out later. Ciao."

Jim stared at the phone, somehow expecting a better explanation but unsure why he should. The sheer hubris of the megalomaniacal idiot was astounding. With heroes like the Crimson Crusader, who needed villains? He was locking up bad people, but he was disregarding the justice system. The charges wouldn't stick, and it would be a matter of hours before the villains were out walking the streets again, committing more crimes.

CC is just as bad as his foes, if not worse. How has it taken me three months to realize that? And who's to say when CC will get bored and decide to turn his powers to evil ventures? What we really need is a way to stop the Crusader, prevent him from continuing down such a dark path.

"What did he say?"

"Huh?" Jim looked up at the owner, who was watching him skeptically.

"Did he tell you he didn't do it? Did he lie to you, or did he just ask you to do the lying?"

Jim straightened his tie, which didn't need straightening, and stood a little taller. Whatever the consequences, Jim wouldn't be part of the Crimson Crusader's devious schemes, however altruistic they might seem.

"I must apologize," he said. "CC just explained that he did start the fight." Which wasn't true, but it ought to be. "It was his fault, and he accepts full responsibility. He will pay for the damages and help you rebuild." That also wasn't true, at least not yet.

The owner nodded once and extended his hand, which Jim shook. "Good."

Jim walked back to his car and paused. It was a really crappy car, and now that he'd turned on his employer, he would be out of a job. He turned back to the owner. "I'd be more than willing to represent you if it requires filing a lawsuit."

If I have to mastermind a plan to manipulate the Crimson Crusader's actions, there's no reason not to make a little profit from legal fees. Wait . . . mastermind? That makes me sound like a supervillain. Then again, I'll be fighting a superhero, so I guess that makes sense. Talk about the lamest villain in history; the only powers I could claim are my wits and nobility, with maybe a bit of knowledge of the legal system. I'll have to pick a really good name.

A young man in his twenties strolled out of the store next door. He saw the restaurant, and his eyes widened. "Whoa! What happened?"

"A superhero battle," Jim said.

"Crazy." He turned back to the parking lot and looked around like he'd lost something. "Hey, I think someone stole my car."

"Was it a blue Chevy?" Roberto asked.

"Yeah. You saw it? Did someone steal it?"

Jim looked back at the restaurant. "No, not stolen. Just borrowed." He grinned. "But I'll make sure he pays for all the damages."

FOR WHAT?

DARREL DUCKWORTH

He placed the cylinder down, slowly and carefully so as not to risk cracking the ceramic casing. Releasing it, he kept his hands in place for a second in case it toppled.

He looked in disgust at the way his large hands shook.

As Thunder Fist, I used to have the strength to toss a car at T-Wrecks and knock him on his lizard ass.

Now, he could barely help his neighbor move her dirt-filled planters.

"My goodness, Stanley," Margie said. "You are incredibly strong for a man your age. Even my grandson can't lift those. And he's a plumber!"

"Vitamins," Stan said, using the automatic reply he had used for decades.

Strong? Not anymore.

Just old. Older than he'd ever thought he'd get.

Always thought I'd go down swinging. Not hanging it up.

It was strange the things that finished a superhero.

Muscle Tank had survived hundreds of battles . . . only to die of AIDS.

Stupid poofter. He was the only one who could really challenge me in arm wrestling.

Ms. J-Time quit long before that, when the battle with VerMan caused her to miscarry. She could deal with monsters, madmen, and alien worms . . . but not that. She'd traded her costume for a real estate license and never talked to any of us again. What hurt the most was what she had said about herself:

"I'm not a hero. I'm a victim of my own stupidity."

And Helen.

He felt the ache again.

They had fought side-by-side hundreds of times and fought with each other too often through the years. They'd raised a family together. Then, helpless, he'd watched her wither and die nine years ago from a cancer no doctor could stop . . . the final result of the freak accident that had given a feisty young girl her powers so many years before.

She'd died, and he had hung his costume up next to hers for the last time.

So many gone.

Yet here I still stand, he thought, staring at the planter, seeing grave markers in the dirt.

Why did we bother to fight all those battles? For what? The world we knew is gone. Everything we cared about, fought for . . . everything that seemed to be going in the right direction for a while . . . it's all gotten twisted and used by the greedy and selfish bastards in power. And the people let them do it. Just gave it up.

For What?

The world's gone to shit.

And here I still stand. For what?

Then a cry tore through the afternoon air.

All his senses snapped to alertness, and he spun around, hands ready. He barely managed to kneel to her level before her tiny body barreled into him, shouting out again.

"Grandpa!"

He hugged Ariel tight while she did her best to squeeze his head off with her tiny arms. She looked so much like her mother.

Looking over his granddaughter's shoulder, he saw his youngest daughter and son-in-law walking across the lawn toward them.

"Oh, she is *darling!*" Margie said, smiling down at the little bundle of joy and noise in his arms.

"She's my little angel," he said, picking her up much easier than he had lifted the planter. She weighed nothing at all in his arms, and she never would.

For her, his strength would never fail.

THE POWER TO
KELLY LYNN COLBY

"Gerald, please put me down. My legs have gone numb." Amelia Weatherford clenched the arms of the lawn chair with her arthritic hands. Her legs dangled in the air.

"Of course, my bride." Gerald set Amelia down in the grass of their front lawn, careful not to lean the chair forward and spill her out.

"Bride? You old coot. We've been together forty years." Amelia pushed on the chair to get to her feet. She took small steps until she was sure she had her balance.

The neighbor kids clapped and cheered from the streets. Gerald bowed with a recently renewed sprightliness. A few months ago, his back had been too stiff for him to tie his shoes. Amelia welcomed the return of her jovial husband. He had been depressed since they retired from teaching last year.

"You could do something useful with this newfound power, like clean the gutters or repair the driveway," Amelia suggested, as she shooed the children away.

She readjusted her wide-brimmed hat, ensuring her snow-white hair remained tucked within it. Leaning on one knee for balance, she picked up the watering hose from the ground.

Gerald hugged her from behind as she showered the red and white flowers, sending the heady fragrance into the air. Amelia leaned against him, and his thick head of dark gray hair tickled her ear. Even with his super strength, he managed to hug her firmly without crushing her.

"Hey, Gerald!"

Amelia frowned at the sound of their neighbor's nasally voice. John Bishop lived across the street with his wife and two teenagers. For six years, he had never said more than "Hello, how are you?" with a curt little wave.

Two months ago, when the meteor exploded over Nowhere, Ohio, everything had changed. One in twenty people had developed inexplicable abilities. As soon as the trend was noticed, the government set up the Center for the affected individuals.

John had developed the ability to instantaneously inflate or deflate anything that could hold air. Their newfound commonality had brought Gerald and John closer.

"Not now, John. We have household chores to take care of." Gerald kissed Amelia on the neck.

She giggled like a schoolgirl. He must have sensed her unwillingness to share her husband. The two had been inseparable for decades. She hated him being involved with a new group of people without her.

"I was wondering if you wanted to go down to the Center. I heard they're going to have a speaker from the American Civil Liberties Union to tell us about our rights."

Without looking, Amelia could hear John kicking the sidewalk with his feet. She tried not to be jealous, but her inner green monster flared.

"The ACLU? Maybe for just a few minutes."

Emptiness replaced Gerald's tight hug. Amelia turned off the faucet. She leaned against the peeling siding and popped the hose, one loop at a time, onto the mounted holder. She watched her husband and neighbor cross the street to John's white Ford Escape.

Her jaw tightened, and her breathing quickened. *You should blow up balloons for your wife and leave my husband alone, Mr. John Bishop.*

"Ouch!" Amelia dropped the hose. In her vehemence, she had missed the nozzle on the end and rapped her knuckles smartly.

"Are you okay?" Gerald jogged across their yard and took Amelia's hand in his.

He kissed it as Amelia watched John enter his house across the street.

"I thought you were going to listen to the speaker?"

"John suddenly remembered he was supposed to blow up balloons for his wife." Gerald scratched his head as he led Amelia inside. "Though he oddly could not remember for what occasion."

Amelia's eyes grew. "Really?"

Gerald put an ice pack on his wife's hand and kissed her forehead.

Such an odd coincidence that her angry thought had turned out to be something John had to do. The door opened, and Gerald's keys rattled in his hand.

"Wait? Where are you going?"

"I still want to hear the speaker. I've been trying to get that construction job. They keep refusing me because of my ability." Gerald clenched his fists. "It's fear and prejudice, and it's ridiculous. I could make the job easier. They would hardly need any large equipment. I'm hoping the ACLU guy has some solutions."

"But, Gerald, we don't need the money." Amelia's composure cracked. "There are always protestors at the Center, and lately they've been turning violent. An important visitor will only strengthen the picketers and make them angrier. I can't afford to lose you."

Gerald sat at the table and put his hands on Amelia's. Their warm weight did more to relieve her pain than the ice pack had. She stared into his empathetic blue eyes.

"We do need the money, my bride. Taxes are going up, and our pension is not. We can't afford to buy paint for our peeling siding, the Buick's windshield needs to be replaced . . ." His face drooped.

"We can fix those with our tax return. We could have a yard sale and clean out the garage." Amelia lifted his chin with a finger. "You taught government and history for three decades. What do you know about construction? You might be strong, but you're not invincible."

She ran a finger over a pink gash running from Gerald's left temple to his chin. "You saved that man's life when you lifted the tree off his car. But you missed the splintered wood that carved into your face."

"That's enough, Amelia." Gerald stood, keys in hand. "I can't let your fear stop me from making our life better." He paused at the door, not meeting her eyes. "I love you. I'll be back after the meeting."

Amelia jumped as the blinds smacked against the wood. Her shock morphed to anger as she stared at the closed door. The Buick rumbled to life. Her jaw clenched. Her face flushed. How could he risk their whole future for a few extra dollars?

Mr. Gerald Weatherford, you come back here right now and make dinner with your wife like we do every Thursday.

Amelia looked out the window over the sink as Gerald pulled down the driveway. Her jaw clenched as she watched the reverse and brake lights reflected in the windows across the street.

The white lights turned off, leaving two red eyes staring back at her. Instead of backing out into the street, the Buick pulled forward. Amelia turned around and leaned against the counter. She worried her hands and focused on the door. Did Gerald forget something, or was he returning?

The car engine turned off, leaving the house silent. Amelia jumped at the creak of the screen door. Gerald closed the door behind him without a pause, heading straight for Amelia. He wrapped her fidgeting hands in his large, comforting ones.

Amelia squeezed his hands. "You came back?"

"I can read the transcripts of the meeting later. I need to cook dinner with my wife like we do every Thursday." He leaned in and kissed her lightly.

Amelia froze as Gerald placed a pan on the stove. Those were the same words she had thought when he was leaving. This incident was too similar to John's sudden balloon-inflating duty. She had thought a command, and both men had obeyed.

"Will you grab the aprons, sweetheart?"

"Of course."

She smiled at Gerald's content face. He wouldn't be this happy if he was working against his will. Amelia shook her head as she dropped the green apron over his neck. It had been a stressful few weeks. She obviously needed more sleep.

Amelia stared at her grocery list, her elbows resting on her cart. She walked down the bread aisle, searching for the specific brand of whole wheat Gerald liked. Amelia spotted the light-yellow plastic cover two shelves higher than she could reach. She sighed. The store had moved everything around again.

A tall gentleman held a jar of jelly at the far end of the aisle. Amelia had an idea. As much as she had tried to not think about yesterday, she had to know if the events were coincidences or a power. She squinted her eyes in concentration.

Please get this bread for me.

The man didn't look up.

You should come help an old lady.

Nothing.

That bread is too high. I can't reach it. Come get it for me.

The man put the jam in his basket and continued to the next aisle.

Amelia laughed. She was old enough to know better. No mind control abilities had been reported in the two months since the incident. Plus, Gerald's ability had manifested immediately. Why would hers take longer?

She grabbed a loaf of wheat from the shelf she could reach. Gerald would have to live with this brand for now.

"Excuse me, ma'am?"

Amelia jumped. She looked over her shoulder.

A young man in a red apron and white polo addressed her. "Do you need help reaching a loaf of bread? I would be happy to get whichever one you prefer."

Stunned into silence, she pointed to the yellow-labeled wheat bread on the top shelf. The young man pulled down one loaf and handed it to her.

"Can I help you with anything else?"

"No, thank you," Amelia muttered.

"My name is Julian. If you need anything else, just let me know." The young man bowed his head as he left.

Amelia pushed her cart forward. Was that a third coincidence? Did it even count when she hadn't been talking to the store employee? She hadn't used the shopper's name because she hadn't known it. Did that make the power real, but unpredictable?

By the time Amelia concentrated on her shopping again, she had traveled through several aisles. She glanced at her shopping list, trying to decide if it was worth it to backtrack and get the things she'd missed.

She smiled to herself as an idea hit her. It was time to test this power and stop skirting around the concept.

Julian, will you please bring me a small jar of mayonnaise, a can of cream of mushroom soup, and a jar of asparagus? I'll be in the meat section.

She felt ridiculous, but she had to know. The temperature dropped as she perused the pork chops. She hated this part of the store, but Julian hadn't shown up yet. How long should she wait? What if he had been in the bathroom when she'd asked? What if she was being a crazy old fool for wanting to have a power like her husband?

They had been equals their whole marriage. The last thing she wanted was the balance to shift as they approached their sunset years. He was making new friends and attending meetings without her. He received government documents in the mail that did not have her name on them. Amelia was losing her husband.

Still no Julian. The open coolers chilled Amelia until her fingers ached. She looked through the bars of the cart at her flip-flops. She closed her eyes and shook the nonsense out of her head.

"Ma'am?"

The young man with his crisp apron and soft polo grinned at her. He breathed heavily, like he'd completed a marathon.

"I'm sorry it took so long. For some reason, I went back to stocking the tomatoes. Your list popped into my head. And I couldn't believe I'd forgotten you'd asked me for help." He placed the mayonnaise, asparagus, and soup in her shopping cart. He offered a colorful piece of paper to her. "I felt so bad I went to the manager, and he said to give you this twenty percent off coupon, good for your entire purchase."

"Thank you." Amelia accepted the coupon with the large-print "20%" emblazoned in the center. "You don't have to do this."

"It's my pleasure, ma'am. Please accept my apologies." Julian turned but then turned back. "Is there anything else you need? Help out to your car, maybe?"

"No, no, I'm set."

"Have a great day, ma'am."

"You, too," Amelia called to his back as he headed toward the produce section. "Unbelievable."

Amelia dropped the grocery bags on the table and called for Gerald.

"Just a minute," he called from the living room. "Wanda, I know. I read the transcripts, too."

Wanda Rayford was another retired teacher who had flirted relentlessly with Gerald, but she'd never had a chance. Wanda's power allowed her to turn any object into a different color by touching it. Their shared oddity had brought Wanda and Gerald closer.

Amelia vibrated with excitement. Her ability would even the playing field again and drive Wanda away for good.

"Gerald, come on. Let's go for a walk." She tucked her hand in her husband's elbow and headed toward the door.

"I have to go. Amelia's home, and we have plans." Gerald hung up the phone.

"Saved by a beautiful woman." He opened the door for Amelia. They walked out into the warmth of the early afternoon. "I wasn't sure how I was going to get her off the phone."

"You managed to shrug her off daily at school. I have faith in your abilities."

"So, a walk after the grocery store." Gerald tilted his head, his eyes sparkling. "Don't you normally moan about the agony of shopping and order pizza when you get home?"

"Most of the time." Amelia bumped his hip with hers, mirroring the twinkle in his eye. "This time, I have something to tell you."

"Don't make me beg."

She had to stop herself from skipping along the sidewalk. The Weatherfords waved at some children and their babysitter playing in the street. Amelia marveled at how normal everything looked when she felt wholly changed.

"I have a power, too. I can tell people to do things with my mind, and they obey." Amelia shook her head. The whole thing sounded incredible when she said it out loud.

Gerald stopped on the sidewalk. "Excuse me?"

"I don't know why it took so long to manifest. I'm not sure how it works. But I thought John should blow up balloons for his wife, and then he did. I didn't want you to . . ." Amelia hesitated. She wasn't sure telling her husband she could control him was a wise decision. "I didn't want you to know until I had verified that I wasn't imagining things. I tested it at the grocery store, and it worked."

Gerald rubbed the back of his neck. "It's quite a thing to digest."

Amelia let her feet guide her down the street, lost in her own thoughts. A glance at Gerald told her he was locked inside his mind, as well. The two walked side by side as they had for decades. Amelia smiled. They would be equals again.

The tinkle of bell-like music from a brightly colored truck bounced off the houses. The children stopped their play at the universal call for ice cream. The babysitter stood in the middle of a crowd of children begging for a sweet treat. The young lady shook her head no and waved the truck by. The children moaned and groaned, heads sagging, as the truck sped up.

"You know, this power can do a lot of good." Amelia winked at Gerald's raised eyebrow. "Mr. Garza is going to give free ice cream to those children."

"Sure, he is." Gerald laughed. "Mister kids-are-ingrates-who-deserve-to-pay-double-the-corner-store-prices-for-his-ice-cream? I'm sure he's feeling generous today."

It was Amelia's turn to raise an eyebrow. "Watch."

Mr. Garza, please give a free ice cream to each of these children, and thank them for their prior patronage.

Amelia crossed her arms and watched the ice cream truck screech to a halt a few feet in front of the children. Gerald put his hands on her shoulders. He squeezed as Mr. Garza leaned out the window and motioned to the kids. The cheers of the children filled the street as they crowded around his window with their hands in the air.

"I don't believe it." Gerald kissed the top of his wife's head. "You do have a power."

"You can take me to the Center and show me around." Amelia felt as excited as the children. She wanted to jump up and down and cheer, too.

Gerald looked at his watch. "They close early on Friday. We'll go first thing in the morning to get you registered."

Amelia rested against her husband's chest as he held her and talked about the people she had to meet. Mr. Garza had given every child an ice cream. He waved the young babysitter over. She walked with hesitant steps up to his window. He took her hands in his and nodded repeatedly.

The dark-skinned girl with light-sepia eyes looked familiar. After decades of teaching, most young people looked familiar. The girl accepted an ice cream cone from the smiling Mr. Garza. As the truck pulled away, the babysitter stared at Amelia where she stood on the sidewalk.

Gerald waved at Mr. Garza as he passed by. "He certainly looked happy enough. After being forced to sacrifice profits, I thought he'd be furious."

"The people I affect seem to think the actions were their ideas," Amelia answered her husband mechanically. "At least, that's been my experience so far." The girl still stared at her. Her focused gaze made Amelia uncomfortable, like the girl knew what she had done.

Amelia shrugged off the eerie feeling. Ridiculous. How could anyone know if she hadn't told them?

"Looks like the show's over." Gerald took Amelia's hand and headed away from home. "Let's walk around and see what other mischief we can find."

Amelia let her husband guide her. They were a team again. That's all she'd wanted.

Gerald tugged on her arm. "I love you."

"I love you, too." She kissed the back of his hand.

Amelia ran a finger over her old whiteboard. She smelled chalk even though the school had switched to dry erase a decade ago. She sat in her familiar chair, flipping on the desk lamp. She had convinced the janitor to open the door. Technically, she had not broken into the school, but it still felt illicit. She didn't want to be exposed by turning on the classroom lights.

Why was she here? An anonymous note left by her rose bushes had begged her to meet here before going to the Center. Who had left the note, and why did she feel compelled to comply? A moment of panic made Amelia wonder if that person had the same power as she did.

"That's not the gift I have."

Amelia jumped to a standing position. The wheeled chair flew backward, bumping into the whiteboard. The sound echoed in the empty classroom.

"Who are you?" Amelia could not see through the pitch black outside the circle of lamplight.

A petite figure stepped into the glow. Her smooth ebony skin accentuated her light brown eyes.

"You're the girl from the street today."

"You don't remember me, do you?" Her voice was lower pitched than Amelia would have expected for a young woman. It somehow made her sound more serious.

"I'm sorry. I don't . . ."

The girl sat in a seat in the front row. She tucked one leg underneath her and kicked the other one in a slow rhythm.

Amelia leaned over her desk. "Stephanie Jones?"

"Steph."

"Yes, Steph. You look so grown up." She walked to the front of her desk. "How have you been? Did you ever finish that novel? Wait. Why did you want to meet in the middle of the night?"

"I need your help. I know you can make people do things."

"Steph, that's ridiculous." Amelia hid her surprise by leaning on her desk with her arms crossed.

"I heard you tell Mr. Garza to give the kids ice cream." Steph's voice shook. "I can read minds."

Amelia picked up her purse. "I don't know why I'm here." Filled with irrational fear, she headed for the door.

"Where are you going?" Steph's voice wavered. "Please. I need you."

"Why?" Amelia leaned her back on the door. The moon filtering through the clouds threw Steph into silhouette. Though unable to see the girl's expression, the retired teacher could hear her sobs.

"My little brother, Sammy, can manipulate electronic devices. He went to the Center to register and hasn't been home since." Steph slid down the desk to the floor. "I know they have him, and I have to free him."

With a deep sigh, Amelia dropped her bag. She placed a comforting hand on Steph's head. The girl sobbed at her feet.

"Please, Ms. Weatherford. He's only fourteen. I have to get him out of there. You could convince the guards to release him. Then we'll run away. Somewhere they'll never find us."

Amelia's mind swam. Fourteen. That's the age she loved: freshman. She and Gerald had not been lucky enough to have biological children. Instead, they had had hundreds of students, new classes every year. She couldn't let one of her children wither in such pain.

"Come, Stephanie Jones." The old woman helped the young one.

Steph wiped her face with her sleeve.

Let's go home and share some sweet tea with my husband. We'll help you find your brother.

Steph winked. "I prefer coffee."

Amelia laughed as she led the girl out.

Amelia stared at her reflection in the mirror over the front desk. "Center for the Especially Gifted" hovered above it in bold black letters. She tried to ignore the noise of the protesters in the parking lot. Their presence made it difficult to enter the Center at all. Gerald had said the picketers were a lucky distraction since the three planned to play hero today.

Amelia placed her hands on the upraised portion of the welcome desk to keep them from shaking. Gerald chatted in his confident manner with the woman behind the computer. In the mirror, Amelia saw a man walking up the steps. Another brave soul who pushed his way through the angry mob.

You forgot to turn the stove off at home.

The man scratched his head, then marched down the stairs. That command had worked three times so far.

Steph nodded at Amelia. She sensed her brother. Breaking into this facility would be pointless if he had been transferred to another.

Amelia focused on the secretary. *Your bladder is about to burst. You can trust Gerald. Run to the restroom for some sweet relief.*

The woman behind the counter crossed her legs. Her face flushed as she rocked in her chair.

"Are you feeling all right, Megan?" Gerald's voice took on the protective quality Amelia found so comforting.

"I'm fine." Megan clutched her legs together at the edge of her chair. "I shouldn't have had that second cup of coffee this morning."

"I can watch stuff up here if you want. It's obviously a slow day."

"No, I couldn't." She pressed a button on her headset. "Kiara, can you please relieve me for a minute at the front? Thank you."

Gerald shrugged at Amelia.

You can trust us, Megan. Go take a quick break.

"I'm sure I can trust you, Gerald. But I can't afford to lose this job."

Amelia didn't know what to do. New to her power, she hadn't considered limitations. The plan had been for Gerald to watch the desk and buzz the ladies to the back. If anything went wrong, he was to pull the fire alarm. The whole plan had to be called off.

"I can read minds, and she can influence people's decisions."

Gerald and Amelia stared at Steph.

What are you doing? Amelia thought.

"I'm not leaving without Sammy." The young woman crossed her arms and focused on the door down the hall.

A buzz sounded as a man in a black suit walked through the door. Standing slightly taller than Gerald, the man looked down on the motley crew. "I am Special Agent Riley. Follow me, please."

"Wait. Where does that door lead? The intake is through the conference room." Gerald stepped in front of the women.

"Do you want to see your brother or not?" The man typed in a code on the number pad and held the door open.

Steph walked around Gerald.

"Everything will work out," Amelia whispered. *You can protect me better by following the plan. Wait for my signal.*

She hoped she infused enough confidence into her command. Her stomach churned fiercely.

The hallway looked like any office building from the '60s. Doors lined the walls in a bleak uniform pattern. Each room had a sizeable window, though the blinds were attached to the outside. Keypads by each lock looked anachronistic compared to the linoleum floors.

Amelia studied the stiff back of the man leading them down the hallway. He hadn't said a word since the door closed behind them. She pointed to her head and gestured at Agent Riley. Steph shook her head.

If Steph couldn't read his mind, Amelia might not be able to influence him. Fear invaded her forced calm.

Special Agent Riley, you should tie your shoe before you trip.

The man stopped, bending down on one knee. His hands paused over his slick black loafers. He stood and put his hand in his pocket.

"Amelia, run."

The man pushed Steph. She hit a set of blinds, tangling in the slats. He grabbed Amelia. Pain shot through her neck before she noticed he had a syringe in his hand.

His voice dripped in her ear like poison. "We will have none of that."

The room swam. The light faded. Amelia collapsed on the floor.

"Ms. Weatherford, please wake up."

Amelia blinked. The light hurt her eyes. Tears blurred her vision. She turned on her side to block the light from the fluorescent bulbs overhead.

"Now what?"

"Calm down, Sammy. We have a plan." Steph helped Amelia to a sitting position.

"One that did not include me getting drugged and passing out." Amelia rubbed her temples, easing the throbbing in her head. *Cameras?*

"Sammy disabled them before we got here. He didn't like the suit men spying on him."

"They tried to sneak in listening devices, but I found those, too. I can sense their presence, like a humming in the back of my head." Though Sammy's skin was lighter than his sister's, he shared her sepia eyes.

He sat in a chair, flipping a pen in the air and catching it. His forced nonchalance didn't fool the retired teacher. His foot tapped the floor sporadically. His jaw muscles clenched. The young man was scared.

So was Amelia. She had never watched adventure movies, let alone imagined she would star in one. Taking a deep breath, she dropped into teacher mode.

"Since we can talk freely . . ." Amelia tensed her stomach muscles so she wouldn't waver. "No electronic lock, right?"

"Right."

"As anticipated. Are you ready to get out of here?" Amelia peered through the bottom of the office window. With the blinds on the outside, she could only see the floor, where a set of shiny black shoes stood by the door.

"I don't know if it's safe to use your ability. They were obviously prepared to recognize the signs. And Special Agent Jerk blocked most of my attempts to read him."

"It's all right, Steph. In the chaos, it will be hard for the agents to be disciplined."

Pull the fire alarm, Gerald.

"Okay, message sent."

Steph took her brother's hand, making him stand. She nodded.

A red light flashed in the small office, followed by a clanging from the hallway. The obnoxious sound bounced off the walls, shaking the blinds. Amelia watched the shoes twist and turn.

You must unlock the door and escort us out before we burn to death.

Though she didn't know his name, she hoped his proximity would boost her power over the guard. Amelia released her breath as the doorknob turned.

"Come with me." The man in a black suit pointed a gun at the prisoners. He pushed the three down the corridor.

She had not anticipated armed guards. Amelia didn't know what to do. She was a planner. This seat-of-the-pants nonsense threw off her decision making. She put her hand out to drag along the wall. The texture grounded her as the alarm wailed. Her fingers bumped into an electronic security lock. She stumbled into the wall next to a door.

Steph and Sammy rushed to her side to prevent her from falling. Amelia patted the panel. *Can your brother free the other prisoners?*

Steph's eyes widened. She put Sammy's hand on the keypad, then pretended to support Amelia.

"Move along. There's a fire. We have to get you out of here before you burn alive." The guard shook his gun at them and glanced over his shoulder like he was being pursued.

Amelia and Steph blocked Sammy from the guard's view.

"I'm sorry. Stress is tough on an old heart like mine." Amelia let her jaw drop as she tried to look as weak as possible.

Before the guard could protest further, all the doors in the hallway popped open, and prisoners rushed the narrow corridor.

"Wait! Stop!" The guard picked up his radio.

Amelia pulled the young people with her and blended in with the fleeing crowd.

"This way." Steph yanked them down another corridor. "I can hear Gerald arguing with the secretary. He's about to pull the door off its hinges to get to you."

Amelia gestured to another wall of locked doors. "Sammy."

"Got it." He pressed his hands on a keypad and closed his eyes. A few seconds later, all the doors in the hallway popped open.

"This way!" Steph yelled.

"You can't leave."

Amelia's legs shook. She recognized that voice as the man who had drugged her. Special Agent Riley stood by the exit with his weapon pointed at the crowd. Two more guards blocked the other side of the corridor.

"If you go back to your cells in an orderly fashion, we'll pretend none of this happened." His words dripped with the confidence of someone accustomed to being obeyed.

Amelia took a quick breath at the sudden silence. Someone had disabled the alarm.

Steph pushed to the head of the crowd, glaring at Riley. "You can't hold us against our will. We have rights as American citizens."

"You have a duty to your country. Your will should be to serve it. If you choose not to, you are a threat to American citizens." A smile wrinkled his face, like a snake opening his mouth to swallow a meal. "You can read minds. Will I hesitate to shoot anyone I deem to be a threat?"

Steph's face grayed. She shook her head.

"Now that's settled. Go back to your rooms."

Amelia's mind swam with fear. Everything had gone wrong. She didn't know what to do.

Gerald, please help us. She whispered it in her mind, a prayer more than a command.

The door behind the guard buckled and tore free of its hinges. Amelia's beloved held the door in his grip. "Gerald!"

The guard twisted around and fired at the intrusion. Gerald shielded himself with the steel door. The prisoners in the hallway dropped flat against the floor. Gerald swung the door up, smacking the guard in the upper chest. The man slammed into the door frame and slumped to the ground.

Steph grabbed Sammy and Amelia and rushed the opening. The other two agents weaved their way around the prisoners on the ground. Gerald tossed the door through the glass entrance. More alarms reverberated around the building. The protestors screamed. A few held up their phones, videotaping the incident.

Amelia, Gerald, Steph, and Sammy jumped into the Buick and sped out of the parking lot.

No one spoke a word until they reached the highway.

"Where are we going?" Sammy leaned against his sister's shoulder in the backseat.

"Kentucky." Amelia brushed the back of Gerald's neck with her fingertips. "There's a cabin up in the hills, far away from the government's prying eyes."

"One of my old army buddies owns it. It's not hunting season, so it should be empty."

"It's temporary, Sammy." Steph put her arm across his shoulders. "Until we can find a way to go home safely."

"What about the others? The people we left at the Center? Where will they go?"

Amelia and Gerald exchanged looks.

"That's a good question." Amelia pulled out a notebook and pen from the glove box. She tossed it back to Steph. "Maybe your sister could use her gift with words to make a plea to the country."

Sammy's face lit up. For the first time, he looked like a fourteen-year-old kid. "Your stories are the best I've ever read."

"Can't we just call the newspapers?" Steph tapped the pen on the cover of the spiral.

Gerald winked in the rearview mirror. "Not without something great to tell them."

"You can do it, Steph."

"And I'll make sure it goes viral. I can push the article to the top of all the newsfeeds." Sammy's enthusiasm made Steph smile.

"Okay, I'll try." Steph flipped the notebook open. "But you have to help me, Ms. Weatherford."

"Of course, my dear. And I think you can call me Amelia now."

"And Gerald." He reached over and squeezed Amelia's knee. "We made it, my bride."

"Yes, we did. We're an unstoppable team." Amelia moved his hand up her leg a little.

"Whoa! I can read minds back here, remember?" Steph raised her eyebrow.

The old married couple laughed. The sound of Steph's pen scratching the paper blended with the noises of the road.

Amelia's golden years were not progressing the way she had envisioned. She kissed the back of her husband's hand. With Gerald by her side, she knew everything would be all right.

THE CRUSH

KELSEY DEAN

A crumpled note left on the kitchen counter at Electra E. Phoenix's apartment, March 18, 2022:

Mom—

I'm out. Don't try to find me. I'm not where you think I am, and if you do manage to show up, I'm ready to burn everything. Even the stupid fringe on your new jacket. Which, by the way, I know you bought to impress that bartender. Auntie Lorelei keeps bringing it up, so don't you dare lecture me about not dating because of superhero responsibilities—when you're busy peacocking behind my back.

Maybe I'll be back tomorrow. Maybe not.

Ria

P.S. I hate you.

P.P.S. You're the worst.

A letter folded neatly on Valeria Phoenix's bed, March 18, 2022:

Valeria—

I know. Believe me, I know exactly how hard everything is for you right now. Remember those superpowers you have? Remember how you got them from me? I was fifteen once, too. My mom told me the exact same thing I told you; I didn't listen, and I ended up hurting someone.

Ria, I know you want to date, and I know other girls your age are already dating. But other girls don't have electricity running through them like you do. They don't combust and shoot flames out of their palms. They can't fly. And when they like someone and their heartbeats start accelerating, there are no catastrophic side effects: no blistering, no melting, no fused zippers, no molten braces.

I know you don't want to hear about me kissing anyone, but I will tell you this: When I was fifteen, I liked a boy so much that I ignored the fact that my hands always sizzled when I talked to him and I went for it. When I kissed him, it jolted him so hard that he shot away from me and hit the wall behind him—he cracked the plaster!—and there were blisters on his lips for a week. I really liked him, but after that, he was afraid of me. He couldn't even look at me. And I couldn't look at him either, because I was so ashamed and furious.

I don't want you to make the same mistake. You'll only end up making someone fear you, and on top of that, you'll be heartbroken. Trust me. I'm telling you that dating isn't an option for you right now not because I want you to be my little girl forever (although, to be honest, I do want that) but because I don't want you causing harm to anyone (including yourself). Being a teenager is hard enough without the added complications that future superheroes have to deal with (you know, like the vigilante homework on top of everything for school, and shopping for spark-proof hair products). Don't go and complicate things further.

I'm going to trust that you're currently directing your fury into a place that won't suffer from a little extra destruction. Maybe that abandoned lot behind the old library, or the warehouse on the corner of Fifth and Kennedy. Anyway, I'm not coming to search for you. You know what to do, and I know you wouldn't dare to approach your crush in your current state. Go rage, spit fire, blow something up if you have to, and then brush off those ashes and come home. We're Phoenixes—we do what we have to do to keep on keeping on.

On that note, I think it's time to introduce the next step in your training; I've left a pile of pamphlets for you regarding all the various martial arts available to you. I'm partial to Judo, whereas Auntie Lorelei prefers Capoeira. Anyway, the choice is yours. The physical training is both a great outlet for anger and an excellent way to exercise control over your body and mind. Believe me, as a superhero, you'll especially need the latter.

I won't wait up for you—see you when you're ready.

Mom

P.S. I'm not trying to date that bartender; you know how Auntie Lo is.

P.P.S. But I will admit that I don't mind when he flirts with me.

A greeting card floating in excess rainwater along a curb, March 18, 2022:

> Hey, Ria, I hope you don't immediately burn this card when it finds you, because I put time and effort into both repurposing it specifically for you AND assigning it the duty of tracking your flighty self down. (Don't roll your eyes at that, missy; we both know my time and efforts are valuable commodities.)
>
> Your mother called, and she's feeling down about her parenting skills because you're being a brat. I know her dating rules for you really suck, but it's for a legitimate reason—you know deep down that your mom is super smart and would never put idiotic restrictions on you. Come on, she started teaching you to fly and burn things when you could barely walk. She's not one to hold you back from the world.
>
> Anyway, when you've cooled down and released all your electrical discharge, you should write your mom a nice note because anyone who makes a literal hero feel bad is kind of a jerk.
>
> Love, Auntie Lo
>
> P.S. Don't you dare give your mom any crap about her love life. Do you know how long I've been trying to get her back out there? Since you were born. I'm not saying it's your fault, but I want my wingwoman back.

An open letter left on the kitchen counter at Electra E. Phoenix's apartment, March 19, 2022:

Dear Mom,

I'm definitely not going to be able to say this to your face, but I can write it: I'm sorry. Maybe I overreacted last night, but still—it's not fair. I know it's not your fault that it's not fair, but my whole life you've taught me that our job on this planet is to make it more fair . . . so you can see how that bothers me.

Also, Mom, I'm glad that you told me what happened to you when you were fifteen. I don't want to hurt anyone. (I guess that means you've raised me right.) It's just hard to remember that I can be dangerous to regular people just by being myself. Does being so different ever get easier?

I love you, Mom. Sorry for being a brat sometimes.

Ria

P.S. Auntie Lorelei got this number for you: 332-9066. It belongs to that bartender, and she says that if you don't call him, she's going to give you a real reason to be embarrassed.

P.P.S. Don't be sad that I slept at Auntie Lo's instead of coming home. It's just easier to listen to tough love when it comes from her, you know?

DAMSELS

CHRISTINA ROBERTSON

Robert stood outside, thinking and watching the trees. It was damn windy out there on the landing, but it was the only place he could smoke since the whole co-op had lilified and gone smoke-free. Everyone knew smoking and thinking just went together. But he had to admit it gave him a reason to be out there, where the trees bowed and swayed like servants before a king. He liked to think like that: servants and kings, damsels and regimental officers. He liked to imagine himself a kind of Kipling's Gunga Din: a respected lower-echelon hero, whose true worth would perhaps be discovered posthumously. The cigarette tasted good. He had been trying half-heartedly to cut down. Conventional wisdom said he must stop. He hated conformity.

Sunlight suddenly sliced through the roiling clouds as a powerful rush of air tried to strip leaves from the old elm at the end of the alley. Then everything went calm, in the overacted way of summer weather. Robert, connected with the drama around him, was moved by the hugeness of it all. He took a long drag off his Kent, squinting as his lungs filled. He stared into the gun-gray sky and its Jesus beams, and his heart ached with beautiful melancholy, his mind drifting away on ancient star-crossed quests.

He smoked his cigarette down almost to the filter, then rubbed it out on the brick wall and put the butt in the pocket of his vest. He lingered, feeling the wind toss his hair, watching dervishes of garbage and dust in the alley below. The wind was pushing the boundaries of time and place, making him remember that which he'd never seen, only dreamed or read of. Tales of dark heroes and bleak moors. He thought too about his own past. The impossible journey. The chain of errors that had made him and delivered him to this moment. He examined the ink stain on his middle finger, then shoved his hand into the pocket of his trousers.

He preferred to consider himself, whenever the mood made it possible, as a sought-after, prolific artist, raw but patient, a sharp, benevolent, successful man. All the things he was not. He liked to visualized Aggie, too, as young and doe-like, smitten with him. But when he slipped into his drinker's labyrinth, things would get confused and ugly. Phantoms of a desolate youth tried to steal the scene. Indulging them never did him any good, so he would force them out of his thoughts. He fought the urge for another smoke. Good thing he had left the pack inside.

The apartment was lonely when he reentered. All that existed of their family room was the crunchy old, olive-colored wall-to-wall couch, an upholstered armchair, which he had draped in a sheet after having spilled coffee all over it, a brass floor lamp from his bachelor days, and piles of books. The walls were an empty white, only a few dusty outlines here and there betraying the previous placement of framed paintings and a large mirror that had gone with Aggie when she left. He supposed he could do more with the place, but why?

Robert slept in Pauline's room. He had turned their old bedroom—his and Aggie's—into his studio. His drafting table occupied the space where their bed had been. That was deliberate, even clever, he'd thought when he dragged the huge thing upstairs and into the apartment piece by piece and reassembled it there. Aggie had left the bed, but he'd tossed the mattress down three flights of stairs into the alley and scrapped the metal frame for a few bucks. Aggie had taken the bedroom rug. She had chosen it: *New Zealand wool,* for Christ's sake. Of course, she had chosen him too but had left him behind with the other unwanted things. Worthless things. He was fine with linoleum. He was fine alone.

He'd laid claim to that pathetic contraption of a fold out couch. He'd moved it into Pauline's room, where he could still smell her and see her toys in his mind's eye. He never hung his smoky clothes in her closet or let anyone else enter. He occupied her room, but it would always belong to her—the beloved girl he had sacrificed for her own good. She was to live with her mother now. The loss of her presence pained him greatly and satisfied his need to hurt. He hadn't been a very good father. He'd stood, bewildered, on the sidelines. Aggie had been the one who was there for her.

Robert couldn't help but listen to the forlorn lamenting of the wind as he scuffed back to his table to work. In their apartment building, wind like this had a habit of pushing up the hall stairwell and sneaking beneath the front door with haunting fingers. It was a sad sound, and insistent. As if he were being visited by the ghost of Christmas Past. He snapped the little radio on. Thank God for the inane friendliness of those radio personality idiots. They were annoying as hell, but they filled up space. They spoke so pleasantly. Everything was presented in nice, small pieces and was to the point. Anytime he heard a news item in depth, it made him angry—at the world and all its useless occupants and their never-ending needs. He'd praise the tyrants, envying their menace. They really did something, not just talk, or wait, or pray. They would calculate and carry out body slams and then take a bow before the gasping world.

Robert worked on a panel for the next installment of his weekly adventure cartoon. His boss hadn't been pleased lately. His mind groped vaguely for something—inspiration, perhaps courage. This was how it went. Robert thought endlessly about what to do. If he called upon himself to rise up, he'd only sit longer, motionless at the drawing table, or settling deeper into the armchair. He read—read a lot, even fell asleep reading. In the mornings, he leached heroes and maidens out of himself at the drawing table, amalgams of brave, historic figures he admired.

He mulled over an idea for a graphic novel and how to pitch it to the agent his boss had introduced him to. But he hated the idea of sharing the world of his creation—a better world—with some son of a bitch on a marketing team. He also thought a lot about Pauline, wondering if she was happier, convinced she was better off without him. Or after he'd had a scotch, he thought about how there was in fact no one better for her, the planet being as it was, populated by ignorant slobs. He often watched the clouds out the bedroom window, smoking and waiting for the God he didn't believe in to show himself.

He wasn't mad at Aggie. She had put up with a lot of shit. Years of it. It was almost a relief when she finally closed the door. He'd expected it for a long time—for her to figure out she could do so much better. He suspected she had only stayed the last few years out of pity and a sense of duty.

He supposed he didn't really want to be married anyway. His adoration of Aggie had long since been replaced by a different attraction. The bottle was another woman, one who never criticized or complained or pinned him down with big brown eyes. He couldn't have taken that distraught look on Aggie's face for one more day. It filled him with shame, a weight he wasn't strong enough to bear. Booze had become like an old war buddy who'd carry his pack when he was feeling weak with the shits.

He was getting restless. Memories were taking potshots at him. He went out and smoked another cigarette on the landing before giving in to the urge to have a drink.

The bottle winked at him from the open kitchen cabinet. It was almost empty. *Oh, hell,* he thought, *this wisp of a nip will do me. Don't need to go overboard. It isn't even three; Pauline's not even out of school for the day.* But the inch of rye left him aching for more. Drink had become his comforting mother, his beckoning woman, his forgiving friend. With bleary fantasies shoring him up, he gladly relinquished reality, yet he couldn't shake the self-hate for long. That was when drink became a mercy killing. Why not? Why not let himself go? he often thought. No one would give a rat's ass if he drank himself into oblivion. It wasn't as if he had much love for his fellow man either.

He grabbed the car keys. He'd make the trip over to the big Walgreens across town. He was sick of the young know-it-all at the neighborhood store, sick of his idiotic greeting—"Hey, Bobby-O, how's it hangin'?"—and his ridiculous hipster soul patch. And his inevitable suggestions. The moron fancied himself a connoisseur of all that rotgut on the shelves, some of it no better than cough medicine. Robert wanted a quick, anonymous business transaction. He needed no guidance, no banter. He wanted no reminders that he was a person, a father, a sad middle-aged man.

Walgreens had Irish whiskey on sale. He grabbed a bottle, paid, and left, throwing the brown bag on the seat beside him. He headed out along the boulevard toward a spot he knew at the river's edge where, hidden in an overgrowth of weeds, was the remaining half of a forgotten bench. He'd spent a little time there in the days after Aggie left. Hidden, undisturbed, he could allow the elixir to expand him. He could fill in the details of a life only traced, never completed—a life that should have been. But before he reached the turn in, he had to slow for a disorganized clutch of cars, honking their horns and swerving erratically. What the hell? They looked like blocks tumbling at the hands of a giant baby, spilling across both northbound lanes. This mess might hold him up longer than he'd wanted . . . and he'd left his pack of Kents at home. Shit.

There was some detritus on the road—a box or a backpack. The cars were trying to get around it, maneuvering in a cautious way. A box wouldn't warrant this kind of confusion and delay. Robert was all but stopped in the middle of the road now, and he was irritated. *Hell, why don't they just drive right over the thing!* He fished around in his pocket for a butt he might be able to get a puff out of. The car in front of him angled away, and he could finally see what the goddamn thing was. Jesus Christ, it couldn't be! A *turtle*? Unbelievable. A sizeable turtle was placidly making its way across the busy metropolitan roadway.

Something stilled in Robert. All the noise in him and around him stopped. All the regrets and recriminations and excuses and fantasies became smoke. The sound of the cars, even the clobbering wind, was filtered out, and he was left with pure reflex. Annoying as it was to delay his alcoholic gratification, he had to rescue it. Right there in the confusion of traffic, he put the car into park and turned the hazard lights on.

Now that the cause of the chaos was revealed, he was amazed by the ignoramuses behind the wheels of their vehicles, still trying to beat it around this noble, solitary creature. He got out, waving at the other drivers and pointing dramatically to the weird migrant on the pavement. They stopped. The road looked immense from this vantage point, Robert thought, standing alone in front of the idling traffic. With everything stalled around him, he felt his own exceptional presence. He took a step forward to get a closer look at the slimy devil, both of them creatures out of time and place.

The crazy thing was ugly as all hell. It was positively primeval. Like Frankenstein's monster, it seemed an unfortunate mistake. Maybe more accurately, a brutal twist of nature, an elephant man. Part turtle and part what looked like lizard, it had a rough, ridged carapace and a leathery, serpentine neck, huge scaly paws with thick claws, a ragged beak, and a substantial tail. The damn thing must have been two feet long and wide as a large hatbox. Robert stared at it from above, reining in his restless imagination, which at the moment was dying to run free. Where had he seen this monster before? He wanted time to sketch the glorious, disgusting audacity of it! But now that he had brought all the traffic on the boulevard to a standstill, he had to do something. Panic set in. Sobriety didn't help. He rubbed his jaw and started shaking.

"Damn you," he muttered down at the thing and at his own burdensome sense of responsibility. Undeterred, the hideous turtle continued plodding, agonizingly, mechanically, following its cockeyed internal compass. A car honked impatiently. "Damn you, too, you heartless son of a . . ." he said a little louder, shooting a disparaging look at the closest windshield. He'd like to see any of these lightweights get out of their climate-controlled sedans to take on this awesome Godzilla. That's right. No one.

He reached down, instinctively avoiding any scaly, spiky, nasty parts. Placing his hands far enough from the head to avoid potential disagreement with the thing, he picked the turtle up by the edges of its ridged shell. Immediately, it withdrew into itself. In a shot, it reached out, aiming for Robert's fingers, beak open, eyeballs rolling. Luckily, it just couldn't reach, but the jolt of the surprise attack almost caused him to drop it. The thing had to weigh thirty pounds. He lifted it to show the candy asses in their cars the holy grail here, the one they were too lazy to liberate. Then he slowly crossed, deliberately taking his time—as much for dramatic effect as personal safety—before reaching the park, where a narrow branch of the river all but stagnated. He deposited it there and for a moment watched the grass part as the magnificently repulsive beast lumbered toward the water's edge.

Snapping turtle. He remembered home, Indiana, and his mother telling him not to swim in the pond beyond the Olbersons' because the snapping turtles would bite his toes off. Robert shivered. He might have lost a bloody hand! And they were carriers of all types of heinous bacteria, as he recalled. He exhaled. Now he'd have to find somewhere to wash. Certainly not in this cesspool, he determined, gazing down at the sheen of green scum upon the water. The thing must have been journeying away from this shithole to find a place to deposit her eggs. What a mother will do . . .

He supposed he had created just such a shithole for his own child. It was a noble thing, he decided, to have let them go. Pauline and her mother were on their journey to a brighter life. It was all tragic, and yet somehow beautiful.

Still shaking, he walked back over the lawn that stretched between the river and the road. Traffic flowed around his car again. His weathered blue Toyota had replaced the turtle as the obstacle there. Some nice people slowed enough to allow him to jog over and get in. He knew he shouldn't really touch anything, so he used his elbow to turn the hazards off and grabbed an old gas receipt to turn the key with. He drove using the ball of one hand, not quite remembering where he had been headed to begin with.

After a few blocks, Robert pulled into Demos' Charburgers to wash his hands. Jittery with adrenaline and inexplicably hungry, he ordered a burger with mustard and onions. And fries. What the hell. He remembered he used to like vanilla milkshakes. He ordered one. He brought his food in a bag to the car. He felt excited, like when he had a good action sequence going for his strip. Like when he read tales of Lawrence of Arabia or Lord Mountbatten or the bloody histories of Viking conquerors. He wanted to tell Pauline about his adventure, his mission—the great turtle rescue.

He pulled a pen from the breast pocket of his vest and began sketching the monster in different poses, using the back of a Jiffy Lube flier he'd yanked off the windshield. When he ran out of space, he tore open the brown paper bag from Walgreens and smoothed it out. He added himself into the scene, saving the turtle and battling a hoard of oaf-like assassins in cars. He drew himself in the chain mail of a knight, adding in his thick-rimmed glasses at the end, a humorous touch. He couldn't help chuckling. She would like this story, his Pauline. He would make her a poster of her old dad saving the snapping turtle. But with a twist. The monster turns out to be a beautiful princess under the cruel spell of the horrible Green Scum Queen. Yes!

He set the car in motion and sipped on the vanilla milkshake as he drove. It was flavorful in a phony way, but satisfying. His mind was alive with beautiful and horrible possibilities. He turned east and headed for Archbold's Art Supplies to get the right materials and colors: India ink for the sky and the creature's dark shadows, metallic gold for the gown of the princess restored.

SABRED

SIR ANDROSS DRANEG

"I am Sabred. This is Longar, my squire. We've been sent to take care of the dragon problem."

Captain Elsau ra Dranolag gazed with disbelief upon the scrawny, squeaky-voiced youth before her. Beside him, the squire, sporting a mop of brown hair that covered his eyes, looked to be equally pathetic.

The battle-hardened crew of the *Andelip*, her flagship, filled the audience chamber with laughter, pointing at the thin nobleman who'd introduced himself. Captain Elsau raised a hand to indicate she would speak. The room quieted instantly.

"Lord Sabred," Captain Elsau began. "I'm sure your lord father, whoever he may be, would not wish to see your life ended." She leaned forward, gifting him with her most condescending stare. "Space dragons are ferocious and cunning creatures, not to be faced lightly."

Snickers ran through the crew of Intergalactic Alliance Peace-Keepers as the lanky youth approached the captain's chair. There amid the muscular men and women of the corps, this unfortunate nobleman looked ridiculous. *Why would they send me such worthless warriors?*

"I am Sabred," the lordling announced once more. "Son of Zeva, Earl of Udeep, from planet Jorn." Captain Elsau rolled her eyes. "I have fought many battles—"

Laughter erupted, but the youth plowed on. "And while I may appear weak, rest assured I am more than capable of handling this problem for you. My uncle, Prince Sain ra Aulden, would not have sent me to you if it were not so."

Captain Elsau's eyebrows rose. The reputation of Prince Sain's rule over the principality of Aulden on planet Jorn filled most news outlets and had done so for the past five decades. *Can this insignificant lordling really be worthy of his uncle's confidence?*

With a resigned sigh, Captain Elsau measured out her words. "Lord Sabred, if you believe yourself capable of undertaking this mission, I suppose you are welcome to try." She paused, settling back into her chair. When she spoke again, it was with unequivocal firmness. "Be advised, however, that I will not provide you with any of our crew for this endeavor. You will face the beasts alone."

"That is not a problem." Lord Sabred's gaze circled the room. Captain Elsau noted the defiant gleam in the boy's eye. "All I require is that you allow me to room on board your ship and use your training facilities. Then, four weeks hence, drop me off on an asteroid in the Daken system."

"Lieutenant Nataya," Captain Elsau called to her most trusted officer. "Make Lord Sabred at home in the officers' deck and see to it he has access to whatever he may need . . ."

Sabred stood in the weight corner of the ship's dojo, deadlifting a load of over nine hundred pounds.

Lt. Nataya stared. "Oh, wow!"

"I want!" Officer Dali spoke in a lusty whisper beside her.

Nataya turned and smiled. "Who would have thought it possible . . . from him?"

"He's rich, too!" Dali grinned, pulling her chocolate brown hair up into a tight bun. "He might be able to kill those dragons, after all." With a cheeky smile, she sashayed toward the aerobics room in a roundabout path that lead her past Lord Sabred.

The smile he gave Dali elicited a grimace of disgust from Nataya. She made her way purposefully across the room, her long blonde hair swinging in its pony tail. As she did so, Nataya snuck a look at herself in the mirrors off the side wall. Her ebony skin glistened with the light perspiration from her time on the jogging track. It irked her how her athletic physique was accentuated by the skin-tight regulation exercise clothes. It made it harder for the men under her authority to take her seriously. Ignoring all the others in the area, Nataya went straight for the bench press. Grabbing the weights, she added one hundred thirty-five pounds to the bar.

Sabred continued his workout, showing only minimal signs of exertion. She watched him surreptitiously. He wasn't unpleasant to look at, she decided. His thin, lean body belied his strength, but it was well proportioned. Tall, with fair skin, jet-black hair, and piercing blue eyes, he had the classical beauty of a sculpted masterpiece. An energy often glowed around his person, especially when he was doing things that required mental or physical strength. She'd seen this in the Rajin from her home planet, but she had never noticed it around a non-ordained individual.

"Would you like me to spot you?" His reedy voice broke through her reverie.

"Not necessary." Nataya straddled the bench and fell back. She smiled. "But thank you."

He nodded and wiped the sweat off his face with his towel. Nataya concentrated on her own workout. As she went about it, she was keenly aware of his movements. His strength and endurance were beyond anything she had ever seen.

"See you at lunch," he said, passing her as she prepared to deadlift her max of one hundred fifty-five pounds.

"Yes," she called after him, watching as he strode confidently out the dojo.

"Come sit with us."

Dali waved her over to their usual table. Sabred and Longar were there already.

As if I would sit somewhere else. They'd spent the past four weeks listening to Sabred's stories, watching him train, and helping him research the bizarre development with the dragons. It had not taken the warrior long to realize what they were up against.

"So, what's your plan?" Nataya asked, taking her regular seat beside Dali, opposite Sabred and Longar.

"First, we'll set up base on the outer asteroid, Gog." He took a swig of his ale and smiled. "Then, we'll track down where the rage of dragons is living, follow them back to their lair. It has to be one of the larger inner rocks."

"I'm still amazed everyone missed the signs!" Dali exclaimed.

"Lord Sabred was able to see the truth thanks to his tech skills with those quantum monitors." Longar, who rarely spoke, praised his master.

Nataya had, at first, barely noticed the youth who'd been introduced as Lord Sabred's squire. At fourteen, his short stature and lanky build made the boy unremarkable. His curly hair hung over his eyes, but Nataya knew the look of adoration they held by the tone in his voice.

"You recovered the footage, Longar," Sabred stated. "It is thanks to you we discovered the dragons had formed a rage. What a remarkable alpha they have coalesced around!"

"He's twice the size of the largest dragon in the known universe," Dali commented.

They'd estimated the alpha's wingspan to be about sixty-plus feet from tip to tip with wings fully extended. Lengthwise, the creature had to be a minimum of eighty feet, from the end of its snout to the tip of its long-spiked tail. It had been tough to come up with the assessment. Longar had postulated it based on the beast's size relative to the Gelderian 747 freighter spaceship the dragon had been spotted next to on the quantum cam.

"A fine specimen," Sabred said.

"A proper way for a warrior to meet death." Nataya's tone held a slight note of mockery.

The knight's code called for valor and an honorable death. The stupidity of seeking one's end in some bloody battle had always disgusted the lieutenant. All faces turned to her. She felt a twinge of regret at her acrid comment.

"Look, I get that you are mega strong and you come from a long line of cunning military strategists and warriors, but why would you want to face a dragon of that magnitude?" Nataya locked eyes with Sabred. "I mean your knight's code and all that mumbo jumbo about honorable deaths; is that really what you . . . ?" Her voice trailed off at the odd look that came into his blue eyes.

"Nataya," Sabred began as he rose. "I will kill the alpha, disband the rage, and return to Jorn unscathed. The knight's code doesn't require me to die. It requires me to live with honor and to defend those who can't fight for themselves. That is exactly what I am doing." With a respectful nod, he strode away.

"Nice going, Nat!" Dali said, as they watched Sabred, followed by his squire, exit the dining hall.

"He is going to die." Nataya felt her anger at the silly nobleman subside. An empty void was replacing it at the thought of a universe without his life force in it. "The least he could do is think twice before going off alone to fight against that creature."

Nataya got up, dropping her barely touched tray of food on the conveyor belt that would take it back into the kitchens. Once in the corridor, she turned toward the captain's chamber. During the time she'd been assigned to help Sabred, the lieutenant had come to one undeniable conclusion: he could win, but not alone. Her mind made up, Nataya knocked on the captain's door.

"Enter."

"Ma'am," Nataya began as she stood respectfully before her superior in the Spartan suite. "I would—"

Captain Elsau turned from typing her captain's log. "Lieutenant, the answer is yes."

"I'm sorry?"

"You came to volunteer to follow Lord Sabred on his suicide mission against the dragons." The captain's gaze held hers. "My answer is yes. You may go with him."

"How—"

"It is evident that you and he have bonded. Officer Dali was here earlier today to make the same request. It followed you'd be coming by soon."

"I think he can do it," Nataya stated. "With help."

"Maybe." The captain rose and crossed to where Nataya stood just inside the door. "We've been ordered to stand on alert by the wormportal. As vessels enter the system, we are to escort them to the midpoint, from which a second convoy will guard them past the system or to their destination."

"Perhaps we'll meet in battle, then, Captain."

"Most likely." Captain Elsau placed a hand on Nataya's shoulder. "Take care out there. *Acta Non Verba!*"

"*Acta Non Verba!*"

They stood, four souls on an empty asteroid, watching the *Andelip* depart.

"Where do we start?" Nataya asked.

Sabred pointed to the raised rock shelf that formed a makeshift shelter. "That cave-like cut should be a good base of operations."

Collecting their equipment, they headed over. The gravity-maker units of their spacesuits made the trek easier, though they still bounced a bit on the uneven ground.

"I'll set up the perimeter," Sabred said upon arriving. "Nataya, set up the atmosphere-creator. Dali, set up the armory in that nook there. Longar, get the living quarters organized over there."

They mobilized. In minutes, the Spocat's energy field had created a barrier between them and the asteroid's gases. The Atmogo unit pumped fresh oxygen into the space and cleansed their carbon dioxide, converting it back into oxygen. Once inside the protected bubble of breathable air, with their gear stored and bedding set up, they sat in their new dining area. No longer encumbered by spacesuits and with the Spocat's gravity field in place, Sabred reviewed the plan with his team.

Sabred floated near the wormportal in his PRAT suit. The space pack's boosters activated occasionally to keep him in place.

"I hate these kinds of missions." Dali's voice came through on his helmet's com, distracting him from his thoughts. "They're so boring."

"Stay alert," he encouraged her. "They may send a scout. We want to track them, so be ready to tag the first one you see with the homing beacon."

"I'm watching."

He looked up and noted she was waving at him. She and Nataya flanked Captain Elsau's ship. The other seven MV-P259 class battleships had taken up positions between the portal access and the asteroid field. Sabred's confidence strengthened as he considered the quick maneuverability of the war vessels. Each carried twenty-seven hundred kapers, both officers and soldiers.

"We should have filled our suits with a snack shake," Dali grumbled. "I'm getting hungry . . . probably from the boredom of waiting for *something* to happen."

"Too late now," Sabred commented. He looked down at the access display on his right sleeve. The monitor showed Dali had switched them to a private com. Sabred frowned. "Keep the communication open so we can all hear if the ships spot a dragon on their detectors."

"Oh! Yes!" Dali's voice implied she had not noticed the change. "Sorry." A giggle echoed in his helm.

Sabred sighed and returned his attention to the black void of space before him. He was certain, after plotting each of the previous sightings of dragons, they were somehow using one of the larger asteroids as their home. He'd considered scouring the field, but it was way too densely populated for such a strategy to be effective. It would simply take them too long, and he wanted to end the threat of attack in this sector as soon as possible.

He glanced past the ships. The gas giant, Daen, looked like a tiny moon from this distance. It served as the midpoint on the trade route through the Daken system. It was there that previous attacks had taken place.

They'd made the journey to Daen and back four times today. The first jump had ended when they led the passenger vessel from Gelderant to the resort moon of Lota, which orbited the gas giant. Sabred's hopes for a confrontation with the dragons had been high, as they would be spending some time in the area. Yet the trip had proven uneventful.

The next three had been fast transfers, as the destination of each lay on the other side of the system. Captain Falterg and his convoy had smoothly taken over on each of those occasions.

"How long do you think it will be before we finally have a dragon sighting?" Dali burst in once more.

Nataya answered her this time. "Could be days before we see action. Who can tell what a dragon rage's timetable is like or why they attack?"

"Indeed," Longar concurred.

Sabred shook his head. Dali certainly was beautiful. Yet the cloyingly sweet attempts at seducing him were off-putting. He'd resisted the idea of letting the two kapers join their mission. Nataya had refused his refusal.

A grin wreathed his face at the thought of Lieutenant Nataya Eno of planet Fratern. The beautiful warrior, with her well-toned, muscular body, took his breath away. Like everyone else, she'd looked down on him at first, believing him a weakling. The look on her face the first time he'd deadlifted had been priceless: surprise, followed by awe and respect.

Captain Elsau's voice broke in. "A ship is making the jump from the quantum stream in ten, coming into sector 2-5."

"Check positions and be ready," Sabred commanded on his team's private frequency.

"Copy," Nataya and Dali came in almost in unison.

"Check, my Lord," Longar responded.

Sabred activated his thrusters, moving into the safest point for following the vessel. The D-Class Alluvian cargo freighter *Yadram* exited the wormportal with a slight jolt. *A rookie pilot must be at the helm.* Sabred hoped that was just for training purposes on quantum exits, and not for the whole journey. He needed an expert to make the coming battle with the dragons less dangerous to everyone. He chuckled to himself as he imagined Nataya's rolling her eyes at the absurdity of his thought.

The cargo ship's bulky body resembled a blend of Jornian sagul and Threan humpback whales. It had a thick, wide middle, with short fin-like wings in grey-black metal forged of double-honrol sheets. The metal alloy's strength made for the perfect protection from pirates, but it would not hold up against a dragon. One puff of dragon's breath would freeze the hull, causing it to become brittle. The sharp talons would then have no problem punching through.

"The freighter is headed to planet Oreh. Should be a nice smooth transfer," Captain Elsau announced.

The seven military vessels of her convoy checked in as they moved to flank the freighter. Captain Elsau's *Andelip* led the way.

"Okay, everyone," Sabred addressed his party. "Stay alert. Remember, the goal is to tag them so we can follow them back to their lair. Of course, if we need to kill some, do what you must, but we have to get at least one homing beacon secured."

"We're ready," Dali pronounced. Her sentiment was echoed by the other two.

"Ladies, take forward positions with the *Andelip*. Longar and I will take rear guard and keep a look out."

"I'm ready, my Lord." His squire's voice held a mixture of excitement and fear.

"Set coordinates," Captain Elsau instructed, pausing to allow each member of the convoy to prepare their nav computer. "On my mark. We jump in three, two, one."

They entered the quantum stream. For five minutes, red-orange waves flowed all around the ships and his team, their passage heating up the otherwise frozen particles.

"Prepare to exit. On my mark. Three, two, one."

They came to a stop. To Sabred's left, the asteroid field, which orbited the system's sun, drifted along. Planet Daen, in all its green-gray glory, sat to their right. Sabred watched as an outlying asteroid hurled into the gas giant, pulled inward by its wide gravity field. His eyes scanned the area. Time slowed. Sabred's pulse quickened. Yet all was still. Again.

In a few minutes, the ship would be handed over to the second convoy and would continue through the system. Disappointment nestled in his chest. Another pointless journey. He hated to admit it, but just as his squire did, he too harbored delight at the coming battle. *Nataya would grimace if she heard me say that aloud.*

"*Andelip,* this is *Horast.* We are under attack. Repeat. We are under attack."

"All ships to quarters!" Captain Elsau commanded. "*Yadram,* speed forward. *Taliho* and *Blaster,* cover it. Get it to safety. All others, kill these monsters! Keep them off the freighter."

Sabred turned his head toward the *Horast,* the last ship of their group. A thin frost covered a portion of the craft's hull. Gas vented from a puncture, the metal edges bent inward. An emerald-hued dragon head, sporting a pair of large curved horns above the ridged frills that framed it, materialized as the creature came out of camouflage mode. Its long snout breathed ice upon the battleship, while the long talons of its hands and feet ripped at the hole it had made.

Three more dragons emerged from the barely perceptible undulations that had warned of their presence. Sabred pushed aside the fleeting question of how they could avoid detection by the ship's systems for a later time as more beasts flanked the military vessel. Two others now clung to the besieged warship. The first dragon reached into the ship and pulled out the body of a dead soldier.

The energy blasts from the craft's topside gun turrets pinged off the animals' metallic scales. The beasts' speed startled Sabred. He'd thought they would be slow, lumbering. But then, their huge size was no problem in the weightlessness of space, he reminded himself.

The five battleships had made their turns, aiming at the creatures. The freighter picked up speed, its escorts coming in close for the jump. The dragon rage concentrated on the one battleship, leaving the fleeing cargo vessel and its two bodyguards unperturbed. Sabred noticed Longar boosting forward. His erstwhile squire headed straight for the nearest dragon, his tag-gun at the ready.

The freighter was safely away. Sabred noticed the flash of red on the periphery of his vision. The other peace corps vessels had opened fire on the various dragons attacking one of their number.

"Longar," Sabred called out on the com. "Watch out! The convoy's attacking."

"Copy, my Lord," Longar responded, maneuvering away from the fray. "I'm going to wait for one to detach and flee. Then I'll tag it . . . I hope."

"Excellent plan," Sabred approved.

A reddish-brown dragon appeared. At ramming speed, it thrust itself toward the ship, its sharp five-foot horns impaling the sides. The internal explosion of the engine shook the *Horast*. Dragons feasted on the kapers as their lifeless bodies floated out of the new breach.

Sabred spotted Nataya fighting a sapphire-blue dragon. The beast was trying to hook onto Captain Elsau's main vessel. Despite the turret fire and Nataya's own mega-blaster, the creature remained unscathed. Its mouth was opening. Soon, ice would flow out upon Nataya and the ship. Sabred activated his ginmra with a single thought. The liquid honrol extended, forming a double-edged sword. The hardening metal glowed green with Sabred's energy.

He headed to the *Andelip*, swinging his ginmra forward. Sabred took position between Nataya and the creature's open maw. Ice burst forth, hitting the blade of his weapon. Frozen crystals sputtered off, floating away. Sabred used all his power, drawing energy from the dragon's own body to keep his weapon strong. Channeling the dragon's breath with the ginmra, he kept Nataya, and the vessel, safe.

Longar appeared behind the beast. With a quick spurt of his boosters, he pulled in close to the dragon's head. The tag gun made contact with the soft flesh behind the dragon's left ridge frill. The beast stabbed with its horn, nearly impaling Longar. Sabred breathed a sigh of relief as he watched his squire retreat to a safe distance. The dragon shook its head.

Something drew the beast's attention. Its long bat-like wings moved to the sides of its bulky body. The tips released some kind of gas, driving the dragon forward. The other creatures were falling in line as well. They headed off, toward the right, away from the asteroid field. The ships maneuvered to give chase, but the bodies were camouflaging. For a moment, slight undulations could be seen, then nothing.

"Where did they go?" Captain Elsau demanded.

"We aren't picking them up on our detectors," someone responded.

"How can that be? Do dragons have cloaking devices?"

"I don't know, Captain."

Sabred turned to look at the *Horast*. It listed like a lifeless bird, its inert body pulled toward the gas giant's embrace. The *Ecil*'s crew launched rescue pods to recover survivors. A mini-salvage frigate from the *Pelin* attached to secure weapons, ammunition, and other supplies. Once these tasks were completed, the captain of the *Horast* would set the self-destruct, scuttling the vessel.

"We're live!" Longar declared, coming up to him and extending the tracker.

The bleep on the screen made Sabred smile. Nataya and Dali came to them.

"Well, any luck?" Dali asked.

"Longar got the tracker in place." Sabred watched the space coordinates on the screen as the red dot moved at a fast pace. It was entering the Daohen moon. Looking at his companion's faces, Sabred smiled. "Now, my friends, let's hunt dragons."

Daohen turned out to be a rocky satellite in orbit around Daen. Its thin atmosphere, due to extreme volcanic activity, was highly inhospitable to humans. But it was a real paradise for dragons. Sabred's guess that the lair would be found on a larger asteroid, where the beasts could live off the gases, had proven false. *I should have known.* The asteroid field's orbit would have led the dragons around the entire system. Had he been right, the attacks would have manifested throughout Daken, not just in the midsection of the trade route. *How did I overlook this fantastic moon?*

Upon confirming the tracking beacon was on the dragon and this was the location it called home, Sabred had sent word to Prince Sain. The Intergalactic Council, at Sain's behest, had given commander status to Sabred and ordered Captain Elsau and her convoy battalion to assist in purging the dragons.

After a tense conversation with Captain Elsau on the role he'd assigned her ships, Sabred gathered his team with the head of the newly arrived contingent of knights. With the holopro projection of the moon's surface, they discussed the ground attack.

"There are groups of dragons around pools of water here and here." Sabred pointed out the spots on the holomap.

Nataya leaned in, cocking her head as she inspected the live feed images from the reconnaissance probes. Three had been placed in orbit around the moon.

"They seem to live in caves on the sides of the volcanoes," she stated, pointing to the beast that had flown up and now disappeared into the mountain's side.

"Dragons like the warmth," Dali added. She twirled a strand of long brown hair around her finger absentmindedly. "Which one looks like an alpha?"

"None." Sabred's voice was firm. "All these are likely followers only. The question is, where would the alpha make its home?"

They all stared at the map. Sabred gazed across the moon's volcanic surface. A creature as large as they had postulated the alpha to be would require a significant amount of space. There were several extremely tall and wide volcanoes along the west-to-east midsection of the planet. However, these were active, and Sabred realized the lava content would be an issue for the alpha dragon.

"Perhaps we should split up and methodically search the moon's main caverns. If we focus on the pockets where we see the most beasts, we may come upon the one we are looking for," Sir Eriq Seller suggested. A Dravidian, the newly knighted youth exuded excitement. Sabred had been pleased to note he was among the retinue sent for the mission. Already, Sir Seller's skills had earned him a reputation. Sabred was certain he would go far. *Too bad he is Dravidian*, Sabred thought.

"The moon is small, but not that small." Sabred shook his head but smiled encouragingly at Sir Seller.

Silence fell on the gathering. Longar pointed to the Falls of Emor, which took up a vast space in the very center of the moon's single landmass.

"The Falls and the pool they form at the base of the plateau are the deepest sources of water. If my research is correct, beneath the plateau lies the great Cavern of Dao. The Falls feed it, as well as the exterior lake. I would think the alpha would be most at home there."

"A good possibility," Sir Seller agreed.

"But then you have the Tri-Hill Canyon farther north to consider, too." Nataya zoomed in on that area. "It has a cascade that feeds the lake on the valley floor. And I see an inordinate number of dragons around. I mean, more than in other places."

"Truth be told," Sir Seller commented. "The alpha could be in any of the millions of caves. The whole moon is filled with mountains. From the scan, it appears there are groups of dragons scattered across the whole satellite. How can we narrow down the lair?"

Silence blanketed the chamber once more. Sabred stared at the map, willing it to give up the secret hideout. There were too many possibilities.

At last, Sabred commanded, "Sir Seller, divide up your contingent of knights and assign small groups to attack the various pockets of dragons. The four of us will watch the movement. When the rage is attacked, the alpha should show himself, or at least, there should be some sign of where he or she is."

"I will see to it the knights are ready to go within the hour." Sir Seller bowed respectfully and exited to get his men ready.

"Are you sure we will be able to find the lair?" Dali asked.

"I hope so." Sabred looked at each of his comrades. He smiled reassuringly and headed to his own quarters to prepare. As he made his way down the halls, he prayed for a sign of the alpha to manifest and for the strength to defeat the beast.

Sabred clung to the side of Mt. Emor. The great volcano, situated in the very middle of the moon's landmass, towered over sixty thousand feet into the thin atmosphere. The cave opening lay just ten feet above him. Below and across the satellite's surface, knights led by Sir Seller fought valiantly against dragons. Captain Elsau's ships circled in low orbit, watching.

When the fighting had begun, the thermal image of a beast under the Emor Plateau had become evident. Convinced this was the alpha, Sabred and his group had landed there. The lair lay beneath in the Cavern of Dao. The band of warriors had soon discovered the only access was through the cave and the steep passageway down into the earth.

"We're almost there!" Sabred called through his helmet's com. They wore honrol armor with oxygen tanks. The volcanic moon's air was too thin to breathe.

"I see it," Nataya answered. She was just below him, to the right.

They continued the climb to the opening. As they reached the ledge, Sabred helped pull the others up. They proceeded down into the dark halls that meandered round the inside of the mountain to the cavern below. Absolute darkness reigned supreme. Sabred led the way. His helmet light illuminated the few feet before him. A couple times, they had to stop and grab hold of the almost smooth rock walls to keep from sliding all the way down.

Eventually, they arrived at the cavern and stood in the threshold. Before them lay a vast area of rock. Six dragons formed a circle around the larger beast. On one side of the cavern, a chasm opened and let in the glow of the red-hot lava from the belly of the volcano. On the other side, a pool of crystalline water gleamed like fire as it made its way out to the larger lake on the surface.

Roars reverberated as the creatures caught sight of the intruders. Activating his ginmra with a single thought, Sabred charged. He felt his companions joining him. Then he was on the first dragon. He slashed at the breast of the greenish fellow as the creature's mouth came toward him, open and ready to swallow him whole. Sliding beneath the beast, Sabred cut a deep gash into the belly, the silicon-metallic scales burning inward at the ginmra's energy pulse.

A second dragon attacked. Sabred turned in time to deal a blow to its protruding maw. A tail swished, and Sabred jumped, rolling and coming to his feet. Wielding the ginmra, he lunged into the first of the two dragons he battled. His weapon's long, hot blade pierced the neck as Sabred slid under it. Blood spurted out, spraying everything. Not wasting time, Sabred regained his feet and attacked the second beast. Enraged at the death of his friend, the dragon dipped its head and made to ram its mighty horns into Sabred. Jumping out of the way as the jagged blades of metallic bone went by, Sabred brought his ginmra down hard upon the neck. He called forth all his energy into the movement, and the weapon cut clean through.

Sabred heard his friends fighting around him. Looking up, he noted the alpha sat motionless, watching his minions defend him. No, it was a female. Her green gaze fell upon him. She rose onto her back legs, her egg pouch showing. She emitted a piercing cry. *No doubt she is calling more dragons to her for defense.* He ran toward her, ginmra extended, ready to plunge the blade deep into the beast. As he reached her, she plunged down, her sharp talons scratching into his honrol back plate. It held, but barely.

Turning, Sabred slashed at her talons, cutting one of them clean off. A roar of pain and anger reverberated through the long neck above him. Pushing the ginmra into the dragon's scales, Sabred sought to cut her throat, but she was too quick. She evaded and brought her long spike-covered tail swishing forward. As he toppled over it, a blade of bone cut through his honrol armor, slicing the flesh along his side. Searing pain raced through him. He released his ginmra and covered his wounded side, hitting the rock floor of the cavern on his knees. Using his body's energy, he willed the honrol metal back into place to cover his wound. Then, Sabred looked up. She was spinning around, coming at him, mouth wide open. He struggled to regain his feet.

He was in her large mouth. With her tongue, she tried to push him into her teeth as she chomped down. Jumping, Sabred used the flat edge of one tooth to hurl himself down into her throat. Her esophagus muscles pulled him deep into her wide belly. Sabred drew upon the beast's body energy, creating a protective bubble around himself. He splashed into the stomach acid, thankful for his Rajin uncle's teachings. Fighting against the swishing contents, Sabred stood. His protection would not hold for long. He had to find a way to finish her off.

He'd lost his ginmra, and the only weapon on him was a small plain steel dagger. It would never pierce her, even from this side of her hard flesh. *How? How can I kill you?* His mind sought options, finding none. He glanced down at the acid liquid. It splashed about his feet, a greenish-yellow lake. Uncle Zegan's instructions on reforming matter by altering it at the subatomic level came to him. It was a very tricky thing, splitting atoms and reforming them without an atomic detonation. It could be done with enough control over the energy forces of the universe. Rajin Lord Zegan had guided him only once in doing so. He'd almost blasted away half of Aulden before his uncle had taken over. Could he do it now?

Sabred breathed deeply, his feet firmly planted on the squishy stomach floor. He cleared his mind. He willed himself to feel matter. To sense the particles that made up each drop of the acid. Slowly, his mind formed a picture of a long yellow-green blade. With all his intention, he called forth the atomic elements of the substance, reforming it with precision. His muscles quivered from the force of his concentration, but he remained focused. An anguished cry reached him. It was Nataya's voice. Her pain pulled on his mind. He felt an atom begin to slip from him, breaking up. He breathed deeply, blocking out all noise, all thought put to the task at hand. He called the wayward atom back into place.

And then it was there, gleaming before his eyes. A long sword of the beast's own stomach acid. Sabred lifted his hand and wrapped his fingers around the pommel. He slashed it about the space, smiling. With a mighty thrust, he lunged at the wall of the belly, embedding the blade, slashing down, cutting open the dragon's flesh.

What remained of the stomach fluid rushed out, washing Sabred along with it. He slid across the rock of the cavern. Coming to a stop, he turned. The alpha roared in pain, her gut open, her intestines spilling out. Thrashing, she fell, hitting the floor of the cavern. There were ten dragons in the cave now, summoned to defend their queen.

His companions battled hard, already having cut down six, not counting the two Sabred himself had felled.

As their queen died, the beasts cried out. Then they fled, just as Sabred had known they would. He clambered to his feet, slipping a bit on the slimy floor.

"You did it!" Dali shouted in the com.

"Ha, they flee!" Nataya's cry came through.

"Are you all okay?" Sabred asked as he managed to find balance. He turned to look them over.

"My left arm was impaled by a claw, but I don't think it will have permanent damage," Longar stated.

"I have a cut to the side, but I'm fine," Dali commented.

"A couple bruised ribs for sure, but still in one piece," Nataya completed their inventory.

"Good." Sabred took a step. The pain in his side stopped him.

"I see you are not without a scratch." Nataya came to him.

"We'll all need a good bath and medical attention," Sabred said, hobbling over to a boulder and taking a seat.

"Lord Sabred, come in." Captain Elsau's call in his com reminded him the job was not yet complete. There was still the rest of the rage to disperse or kill.

"Yes, Captain. I'm here," Sabred answered.

"Many of the beasts are abandoning the moon. Can I assume you have vanquished the alpha, then?" The disbelief in her voice stung.

"That is correct."

"Well, I suppose we kill as many as we can and allow the ones that get away to go in peace."

"Yes."

"Very well."

"May we come on board? We have some wounded."

"Yes, come aboard," Captain Elsau stated. "I'll let the med bay know."

"Thank you," Sabred said, signing off. Switching frequencies, he called out, "Sir Seller, are you there?"

"Yes, Lord Sabred," Sir Seller responded. "The dragons are fleeing. Shall we give chase?"

"No, let them go," Sabred commanded. "Regroup on board the *Andelip*."

"Copy."

A few weeks later, Sabred prepared to disembark at the space port at Anco City, Dravidia, planet Jorn. Captain Elsau had been ordered to give them a lift back to their planet. She and her crew would report back to the Intergalactic Alliance Peace-Keeper Corps's base on Pelangel once this task was done.

"So, this is goodbye," Nataya said from the doorway of his chambers.

"I hope not." He turned and locked eyes with the woman he had come to love. "If you would allow me, I would like to take you to dinner sometime."

Her beautiful laughter filled the space, her ebony skin gleaming in the harsh lighting of the spaceship. His heart skipped a beat.

"Yes," she said once her mirth subsided. "Though I am not sure what planet we will do that on."

"Jorn." Sabred couldn't keep the joy from his voice. "I took the liberty of having you transferred to the Peace-Keeper Corps squadron that operates out of Aulden."

"Well, now. You were that sure of yourself?" Her eyes held mischief as she approached.

"No," he admitted, having trouble breathing as she drew near to him. "But I had hope that if not now, then in time I might win you over."

"You already have, my Lord."

INVASION OF THE BRAIN-SCRATCHERS
EMERSON ADAIR

Things always happened this way. Gerald inevitably ended up looking after his eccentric older brother. And today was no different.

"Chevron, why is there a toilet seat around your neck?"

Chevron grinned and adjusted the inverted U-shaped seat. The brushed-steel surface was polished to a bright sheen, like some treasured piece of jewelry.

"It goes with my new hat," Chevron said, picking up a clean bedpan, also made of steel and polished to a reflective shine, and placing it on his head. "I got it to keep the brain-scratchers out of my head."

"The who?" Gerald asked. "I thought most people made little caps out of foil to keep mindreaders out—"

"Nah. Those only work on lower-level telepaths," Chevron said, waving his hand dismissively. "Brain-scratchers are much more advanced. But there's something about bedpans. The makeup of the alloy is just perfect to confuse their sensors."

"Right," Gerald said, running his hand through his dark hair. He watched Chevron pick up a cup of Jell-O and wiggle it with a concentrated look, as if inspecting it for quality. "So when are you going to let the doctors do an evaluation?"

"I don't need one. I'm perfectly sane," Chevron replied. He looked into Gerald's gray eyes and held his gaze for several seconds. "I may be the only person in this colony who is."

"That might be easier to prove if you let the docs evaluate you," Gerald said, staring back into his brother's electric-blue eyes. "Ever since you came out of cryo this morning, you've been a few phasers short of a photon."

"Don't use tech-speak, Gerald. You're not good at it," Chevron said. "And cryo wasn't the problem. It was the brain-scratchers!"

"Right, the aliens that invaded your brain and stole all your knowledge," Gerald said incredulously.

"And scratched my mind. That's what makes them so dangerous," Chevron said. "But I did something they didn't expect. I took some of their knowledge, too."

"Oh, yeah? What did you find?"

"Lots of stuff. Lots of plans," Chevron said, glancing around the room as if he were afraid an alien would materialize somewhere nearby. "That's what I've been trying to tell you. I'm not the first victim. There were others, all in cryo. The brain's more vulnerable then. You're sleeping, with no control over waking. That's why so many people have come out acting like brain-dead moonbats. Their brains were scratched."

"So the old man who used his hospital robe to make a turban and walks around naked calling himself an emperor was scratched?" Gerald had to admit Chevron told a good story when he put his mind to it.

"He's not just an old man," Chevron said, lowering his voice as if afraid someone might hear him. "He's supposed to be the colony's head security officer. He knows all the technical specs of every defense system and security grid on this planet. And now the brain-scratchers know it, too. That can only mean one thing."

"Let me guess," Gerald said, "A full-scale invasion of this *pivotal* mining facility."

"Gerald, you're not listening!" Chevron said, shaking his head sadly as if he pitied his short-sighted brother. "It's not the mines they want. I got inside their heads, just like they were inside mine. They want the—"

At that moment, alarms started sounding across the colony. Red lights flashed in the room as a female voice came over the intercom.

"RED ALERT. RED ALERT. UNIDENTIFIED SHIP ON APPROACH."

"Dear God!" Chevron said, staring at the speaker as if it were a herald of doom. "They're here. I thought they wouldn't come for a few more days!"

"Chevron, calm down!" Gerald said, grabbing his panicking brother and holding him in his chair. "It's probably just a scouting ship returning early."

"No! Scouting ships all have autopilots and ID transmitters so if something goes wrong while they're exploring, the ship can bring the logs home!" Chevron yelled, straining to stand up. "Don't you see? They must have known I was lying, and now they've come to wipe us out!"

"Chevron, even if the brain-scratchers are real, our orbital guns should stop them," Gerald said, desperately trying to calm his brother down. "We're safe as long as we're here."

"You don't get it! I'm one of the orbital gun operators!" Chevron whimpered, slumping back into the chair. "The brain-scratchers wanted my knowledge of how the guns worked. They needed to know how to get around them. And they got it. But I found their weakness, too. We have to get to the medical office before they land!"

The door to the room slammed open. A man in the dark green uniform of ground security forces stood in the doorway, a plasma blaster clutched in his right hand.

"Gerald! I've been looking all over for you!" the man said. "A ship we've never seen before is approaching orbit, and we need you back at the base! Didn't you hear the alarm?"

"Approaching orbit?" Gerald asked in disbelief. "What are you talking about, Ford? How did they get past the defenses? Aren't the turrets online?"

"That's the strange part. They just slipped through our long-range sensors. It's like they came out of nowhere!"

"Not nowhere," Chevron said matter-of-factly. "They stayed in warp until the last second, then made an instant drop to impulse."

Gerald and Ford stared at him.

"That's not possible," Gerald said. "There would have been some traces of radiation from the warp engines before they arrived. Warp rifts always show radiation. We should have had at least thirty seconds' warning!"

"That's the strangest part," Ford said. "Nothing showed up on any of our scanners. One minute they were clear, then we're looking at a ship unlike anything we've ever seen before."

Gerald slowly turned and looked at his brother, eyes wide and alarmed. "Chevron, you said these brain-scratchers want something. What do they want?"

"Not much," Chevron said. He was using the cloth belt from his bathrobe to tie his bedpan more securely on his head. "Just some codes from the command computer. Oh, and all the people on the colony to serve as slaves on their vessel."

"What?" Ford yelled. "How could you possibly know tha—AAGH!"

Ford stiffened, grasped his head, and collapsed to the floor. As Gerald reached toward his friend, a lancing pain struck him right behind the eyes and exploded through his brain. He fell, screaming and writhing next to Ford as Chevron ran out of the room. His brother returned with two bedpans, one for each.

The explosions inside Gerald's skull settled down into dull, aching throbs. He had flashbacks to the morning after his first time drinking true Mexican tequila, brought to the colony by a family fresh from Earth. Next to him, he heard Ford's shrieks subside into groans. The men lay on the floor for several minutes, gasping and sobbing, until Chevron pulled them up and sat them on the bed.

"What the hell was that?" Ford gasped.

"I already told you, they're brain-scratchers," Chevron said as he used an IV tube to secure Gerald's bedpan hat. "Now that they're here, they'll be able to disable everyone from orbit unless we can stop them."

"I thought my head was going to explode," Ford said, knotting an IV tube under his own chin and checking to see if his hat was secure. "Do you think that happened all over the colony?"

"It's hard to say," Chevron said. "I don't know how they attack the brain or how wide their range is. We should probably assume they struck some strategic groups, if not everyone. They won't kill us, though. Dead slaves are useless."

"So what will they do now?" Gerald asked, walking quickly toward the door. "What are the codes for? How do we stop them?"

Chevron grinned as he followed his brother into the hall. Finally, someone believed him! "The codes would allow them to access the facility's research database. Do you remember what was happening before I left to visit Earth? Everyone was excited about some unidentified ore they found in one of the mines. The aliens are looking for something similar, and they want to know if what we found is it. If it is, they'll take the ore and all the knowledge our scientists have gleaned, as well as the colony's entire population. If it's not what they want, they'll settle for just the colonists."

They were running down the hall now. Gerald stopped at a split in the hallway. One hall went to the medical offices, the other led to the rest of the colony.

"You said we need to get to the medical offices. Why?" Gerald asked his brother, looking deep into his eyes again, as if trying to read the answer.

"They have a rather . . . unique weakness," Chevron said. "Their technology is advanced, but they've never come across an X-ray machine before. Their bodies are incredibly fragile. Even more so than ours. That's why they scavenge technology, to find a way to compensate for their lack of strength."

"And an X-ray machine is the key? That seems kind of lame for an advanced alien civilization to be vulnerable to such outdated technology," Ford said.

"Indeed," Chevron said. "It's a bit of irony I rather enjoy after what they tried to do to me. And it's especially fortunate that Dr. Willis has been experimenting using X-rays with antibiotic synthesis to encourage regeneration."

"Okay, but how do we use this to attack them?" Gerald asked. "It's not like we can ask them to lie down on an examining table one at a time."

"The orbital guns should be able to penetrate their hull," Chevron said, looking thoughtfully into the space just above Ford's left ear. He looked like he was trying to pull the answer out of thin air. "But there's a problem. If they appeared as close as you say, they're already past the guns. And there's only one person with the clearance to turn the guns toward the colony."

"Who's that?" Gerald asked. He had a sinking feeling he wouldn't like the answer.

"The head of orbital security," Chevron said, looking Gerald in the eye. "And I think we can find a way to defend the colony. I still have clearance to get into the arsenal. The brain-scratchers are past our main defenses, and they will probably take their time making sure everyone is disabled before trying to land. I estimate we have an hour at best, though."

"Great, so what's the plan?" Ford asked. He looked at Chevron as if everyone in the colony's life hinged on his next words. And really, they probably did.

"We're going to make an X-ray bomb," Chevron said. "Gerald, you're the best at handling . . . eccentric people. You go visit the emperor and convince him to join you in the orbital defense office. Ford and I are going to perform surgery on a missile, and then we'll meet you there."

"Great," Gerald said. Somehow, he always got stuck doing the colorful stuff. "And how will I do that?"

"He thinks he's an emperor," Ford said. "Tell him his empire's under attack and he holds the key to its salvation, or something."

"Right. This better work!" Gerald said and sprinted back toward the mental ward.

A minute later, he burst through the door of a room very similar to Chevron's. Only this room contained a naked sixty-two-year-old man with a carnation pink hospital robe wrapped around his head like a turban and covered by a bedpan. The "Emperor" was sitting on the side of his bed, making a speech to a pot of flowers as if it were a holoprojector. Gerald shook his head, sighed, and then put on his best panicking face and rushed to the man's side, kneeling on the floor.

"My Emperor, I bring grave news!" he said, bowing his head. "Your realm is under attack. Invaders have broken our defenses!"

"Indeed, I donned my battle crown as soon as the alarm was raised," the Emperor said in an exaggerated, obviously fake British accent. "But who would dare invade my domain? The Monguls? The Huns? The Greeks? Russians? Romans? Or could it be the diabolical French, those flouncy, overreaching sons of Moroccan monkeys?"

Gerald blinked in surprise and stared at the man for a second. He was much farther gone than Chevron. How could his brother be so lucid yet slightly unbalanced when this man was downright bonkers? Gerald shook himself. There wasn't time for that. He had to get this man to come with him, or all was lost.

"It is a new enemy, My Lord," he said, looking into the man's wild eyes. "One with abilities we have never seen. They could destroy all if we don't act quickly."

"Great Scott! And do you have a plan of attack, General Chang?" the old man asked, glaring down at Gerald.

"Yes, My Lord," Gerald replied. General Chang? He wasn't even Asian! "I and two other generals have formed a strategy that should wipe them all out with one swift stroke, but we need your help to accomplish this."

"My help?" the Emperor asked. "But, General, you are the warrior. I must stay in the palace to give the people hope and strength. I must hold here while you and your brave men lead the fight."

"But, My Lord, the weapon we need is protected by special defenses," Gerald pleaded, grabbing the old man's hand in desperation. "The barriers are made so that only you can disable them. Please! You must come, or all is lost!"

The Emperor sat on his bed as if it were a throne. He looked down at Gerald, his tongue sticking out of the side of his mouth as he hummed to himself, his brow wrinkled in thought. After a few seconds, his face cleared and he stood up, motioning for Gerald to do the same.

"I will accompany you, then, if I must," he said. "Lead the way, General."

"Thank you, My Lord," Gerald said, bowing. "But before we go, it would be best if you put on your robes of state. It will give the people confidence to see their emperor going to war in his finest garb."

"Yes, I believe you are right," the Emperor said, walking to the room's closet. He pulled out a lavender bathrobe with a yellow rubber ducky about the size of Gerald's palm embroidered on the right chest. He dressed himself, slipping on a pair of neon orange slippers and turned back to Gerald.

"Lead on, General," he said regally, holding out his hand. Gerald took it, and they ran down the hall.

When they exited the building, both men froze in shock. The entire colony was silent except for the occasional shriek of pain and terror. Streets that normally funneled people to and from assignments were now full of collapsed, sometimes convulsing colonists.

In front of the building, a security vehicle was perched halfway over the curb, the driver slumped over the steering wheel. Gerald grabbed the Emperor's hand and ran for the machine, but the old man pulled away to crouch over a young nurse. She was lying on her side, curled into the fetal position and whimpering as she clutched her head.

"What is happening to her?" the Emperor asked as he reached down to stroke her forehead. He looked up at Gerald as tears ran down his face. "What is hurting my people?"

"The invaders are attacking their minds," Gerald said softly. "But we can stop them if you come with me to activate our special weapon."

The old man took a deep, shuddering breath, nodded and stood up. He followed Gerald to the vehicle, and they started the careful, winding drive to the orbital defense office.

Fifteen minutes later, they were in the back of the orbital defense offices. There was a security entrance hardly anyone used or knew about. It would be free of civilians and guards. He swiped his card and sighed gratefully when the red light switched to green. They slipped through the door and started running up the service stairs. Gerald hoped there weren't too many people near the orbital defense controls.

On the top floor, Gerald slowly, silently slid the door open. He pulled the Emperor behind him into the hall, which was littered with unconscious men. Their slow, labored breathing was the only sound in the space. Then he heard a familiar voice.

"Ford, check the hall. I think I heard a door."

The familiar shape of Ford appeared silhouetted in a far threshold. "It's Gerald, Chev! He got him!"

"We need to hurry, Your Majesty," Gerald said, pulling the Emperor with him. "The weapon is controlled in here."

Ford shut the door behind them as they entered and shot the lock. The old man looked Chevron up and down, then turned to Gerald.

"Are you sure this man can be trusted?" he asked, adjusting his pink turban. "He dresses like a madman!"

"I trust him with my life, Majesty," Gerald said. "Step over here, please, and place your palm here." He took the old man's arm firmly and pointed to a scanner. "Then you just have to look in this little window, and we will take care of the rest."

"Ah, I see," the old man said. "Guards on the other side who know my eyes, are there? Clever." He looked into the retina scanner.

Within seconds, they had full access to the system. At the same time, a screen taking up half a wall lit up, and an image of the alien ship filled it. A side hatch was slowly opening, and a small landing craft could be seen.

"Looks like they finally decided to come down here," Ford said, reflexively reaching for his weapon. "Hurry up, Chev!"

"I'm putting in the coordinates now. Just one more minute!" Chevron said, punching away at the control screen. The display showed the orbital satellite spinning to face the alien ship. As the plasma gun locked on, the ship began to rotate toward the weapon.

"Great Scott, the enemy is aware of the plan!" the Emperor cried, taking cover behind the desk. "Do your duty, generals!"

"You got it, sir!" Chevron said and held down the big red button on the upper right corner of the console. The gun on the display charged, then shot a monstrous bolt of plasma. The alien ship reeled, knocked sideways by the sheer force of the blast. As they watched, Ford pulled a remote from his pocket and triggered the missile.

More hatches opened, and a flood of tiny ships tried to flee the crippled main vessel, but it didn't matter anymore. The three men watched in triumph as a nuclear missile threaded the needle straight into the alien ship. They stared, stunned, as the ship blasted apart and the growing explosion consumed the surrounding craft. Gerald turned to his brother.

"I thought you said you were going to make a bomb with X-rays."

"Yes, well, we were, but then we saw the nukes," Chevron grinned. "Why kill when you can overkill?"

FLIGHT OF THE CROW
JAE MAZER

The hair around her face fanned out, gossamer butterfly wings
shredded in webs on the glistening asphalt. The silver and black
strands glistened like crystal in the morning sunlight. Warmth
permeated the skin on her cheeks, skin damp from dew and pocked
from the harsh sidewalk. She smiled.

The air was thick with humidity and a plethora of smells confirming
the existence of humanity: food, fuel, waste, sweat. She breathed
deep, reaching beyond the offensive—which always bullied the soft
and delicate aromas out of the way—and smelled beauty. Shampoo,
hydrangea, freshly baked pastries, morning coffee from the barista on
the corner, the ocean. Even the scent of greasy street meat made her
heart flutter.

"Yummy place, this world," she said to no one in particular.

Sister Crow rolled onto her knees, her bones and joints complaining
even under her waifish frame. She rose to her feet, gathered and
folded her blanket, and placed it gingerly in her cart as if it were a
swaddled infant. She kissed her hand and lay it upon the soft pink
fabric.

"Good mornin', love," she said, batting her eyes at the worn, stained
fleece. She'd had the blanket for quite some time—ten years, give or

take—and to her it was as precious as a diamond. And so much more beautiful.

She shuffled down the busy sidewalk, making eye contact with dozens of sets of eyes that refused to latch onto her longing gaze. She walked across the street and made her way past the ferry terminal and down onto the path along the seawall. Once she had found a little nook to park her cart, she plucked Ol' Pinky out and set her on the ground, still folded. She sat on the blanket, and the gentle fleece cupped the boney curve of her wasting buttocks.

"Thank you, old friend," she said to the blanket.

Then she watched. People passed. They looked but didn't see; they raced and dashed and flitted about. And she watched. She watched their routines, their hopes, their drive, their pain. And felt it all. Then watched some more.

"It was never yours and never will be," a shrill voice whined in her ear.

Sister Crow swatted at her shoulder, her face deteriorating to a sullen gloom.

"Be gone, vile thing," Sister Crow growled.

People passing by gawked covertly from their peripherals, for fear acknowledgment might make Sister Crow's plight spread to their own grey matter like wildfire.

"All of that," the voice continued. "All the sensations, the purpose, the meaning. You've never had that in your life. And it's too late for you now. You're just an old bag of bones that's accomplished absolutely nothing."

"Shoo now," Sister Crow said firmly, a mother's scolding wrapped in a fearful whisper.

"You are washed up, a has-been, a ne'er-do-good. And your expiration date is nigh, old crone. I know you feel it. I can smell the stench of your defeat."

Sister Crow drew a steady breath in through her nostrils, then exhaled through forcibly relaxed lips. She turned her head to the side and locked onto two ruby-red orbs, each divided by a slit of obsidian. Dharius had been with her a long time, longer than she cared to remember, parroting the tongues of all her critics, including herself. She kept telling herself that she was stronger than the lies and hatred he spewed. Stronger than suggestions intended to keep her on her knees. He could chatter, but it would never sink so deep as to penetrate her heart. But sometimes . . .

"Resist me, crone," Dharius said, "but you know it to be true. You'll die a worthless sack of meat, leaving a mark on the world as inconsequential as the strike of a wet match. Useless. Pointless. An absolute waste—"

A slap sliced the words from Dharius's mouth. A tiny barbed tail, iridescent and glowing with remnants of moonlight, had snapped around the back of Sister Crow's neck and struck Dharius across his black lips. He gasped in horror, then retreated down Sister Crow's sleeve, crumpled mewls escaping his bloodied jowls.

"Just in time," Sister Crow said, shuddering off the residual discomfort of Dharius's words. "He was on the verge of annoyin' me on this fine day."

Sister Crow looked to her left shoulder, where the faerie perched. Its opalescent eyes glimmered in the sunlight and its lips were pursed in a soft smile. The silver faerie twirled Sister Crow's mangled hair through her delicate fingers, replacing knots with intricate braids just three strands thick. Sister Crow smiled, her heart swelling at the sight of the ethereal little creature. Hair like fire, skin a cold diamond-silver, solid black eyes, and plump ruby lips. She had no name, this faerie companion of hers . . . or maybe she did. The faerie had never uttered a single word in all the time Sister Crow had the pleasure of her friendship. The faerie simply kept Sister Crow company, touching her skin and her soul as the need for tenderness arose. And above all, she illuminated the beauty of the world.

Zara Mickelson hated the taste of her own blood.

She brought a tissue to her lips, avoiding eye contact with the mess in the mirror.

"Why today?" she asked the trembling reflection.

After dabbing the blood from her face, she addressed her appearance as best as she could, spackling on layers of foundation and lipstick to mask the morning's activities. Once she looked like an undercover rodeo clown, she slipped on her blouse and headed downstairs to the kitchen.

"You okay?" Brent asked, his eyes studying the cream-to-caffeine ratio of his coffee.

"Sure," she said, delving right into her morning routine. Coffee, breakfast, pack bag, go. Go. Go.

"What's the rush?" he asked, his eyes abandoning cowardice and leaving his cup.

Go, go, go.

"Meeting this morning with the board. We're trying to get funding—"

"You have time to sit and eat with me," he said, tapping the table with a meaty finger.

"I really can't." Her voice quavered beneath a veil of assertion. "After we . . . I'm already later than I'd like to be."

He sighed.

That sigh.

I'll pay for this later, she thought as she scooped up her things and walked out the front door, leaving all hope of coffee, breakfast, and peace behind.

As Zara walked down the sidewalk to her office, her legs were cement, weighing her down as she tried to traverse the quicksand of life. *Everyone will see,* she thought as she brought her fingers to her throbbing lip.

Everyone will know.

She passed by street vendors and a plethora of pedestrians, blank faces moving along a slate-gray backdrop. *The world is an ugly place,* she thought. Her body was present, trudging toward her professional obligations, but her mind was still at home, gasping for air, drowning in a cyclonic tyranny of authority and domination. Every set of expressionless eyes that fell upon her face reminded her of her weakness, of the apathy of the world around her, and of her constant uphill battle. She moved through each day driven only by the second hand that pushed her tick by tock to the end, whatever end, any end that might bring the futility to conclusion.

Her stomach growled, startling her out of her inner frenzy. She realized that in her haste to escape, she hadn't eaten breakfast. She certainly couldn't add hangry to her myriad of emotions, so she stopped at a street-meat vendor, selecting a spicy breakfast taco she could consume quickly before work. Once the greasy fare was in hand, she wandered across the street, drawn by the gentle waves of the ocean. She walked along the inner seawall, plunked herself down on a bench, and took a bite. The generous helping of hot sauce seeped from the edges of the taco, dribbling down her stinging lip and onto the front of her cream-colored blouse. She looked at the bright orange spot, but her eyes trailed to the surrounding droplets. Minuscule splotches of browning crimson, smattered over the front of her shirt. *Blood,* she thought.

And she cried.

Sister Crow watched the worn and deflated woman stop to indulge in a mobile breakfast before the devastating spill on that fateful park bench. She observed in fascination as the little dribble of pulverized pepper sauce drew an unnecessary amount of tears.

"Spicy, but not sad," Sister Crow whispered to herself. "Spicy is not sad, is it?" she asked the silver faerie on her shoulder.

The faerie twittered with excitement, bouncing and cartwheeling down Sister Crow's arm and into her lap, a trail of light flowing behind her like a bridal train of Christmas tinsel.

"What has your knickers in a knot?" Sister Crow asked, then looked back at the woman on the bench. The woman was still crying, hot sauce on her face and despair slumping her frail body. "I've no time for your energy right now," Sister Crow said, brushing the faerie to the side. "I gotta tend to this missus." The faerie dissolved into glitter, swirling away with the wind like a sparkling dust devil.

Sister Crow started toward the bench but stopped short when she got a better look at the woman's face.

"Ah," Sister Crow said, her eyes dimming. She eyed the woman from head to toe: her professional attire, her fingernails gnawed and picked straight to the quick, the nervous tap of her bargain-basement heels. Sister Crow proceeded to the bench and sat next to the weeping wanderer, so close that their outer thighs touched.

Zara startled at the sudden and unwanted guest who evidently had zero respect for personal space.

"'Tis only a bit o' sauce."

It was a woman with long, straggly salt-and-pepper hair, skin marked with the roadmap of a laborious life, and a tattered old gown meant only for covering the unmentionables. Zara recoiled at the sight of her, but something in the woman's eyes kept Zara's ass planted firmly on the bench.

"I'm sorry?" Zara asked, leaning back but not sliding over.

"Sauce, dear," Sister Crow said, pointing at the hot sauce on Zara's blouse. "And blood, too, but nobody be noticin' that against that fluorescent pepper sludge. Your spill is a blessin', methinks, if you were tryin' to draw attention from that lip o' yours."

Sister Crow brought her bony digit up to Zara's face. Zara flinched and then lowered her eyes to the worn toes of her shoes. Sister Crow withdrew her hand, folding it with the other on her lap.

"Nah," Sister Crow said, her brow furrowed to a fat caterpillar. "Ashamed is foolish. You? You had nothin' to do with that mess. I'd wear that like a badge o' honor. It tells the world you have survived dealings with a cowardly idiot."

Zara's tears turned to giggles despite the funk that shrouded her heart. Sister Crow smiled and raised her hand in the air.

"Now, child," Sister Crow said. "I'm gonna place my hand on yours, and I'm gonna hold it. And you're gonna let me."

Zara didn't have time to argue. Midblink and halfway through a startled inhalation, Sister Crow's hand was around hers, clasping it as a grandmother would. And Zara did exactly as Sister Crow directed. She let her. She didn't pull back, she didn't resist. What she did do, however, was like it.

Sister Crow enjoyed the extended company her new friend gave her. A long overdue dose of human contact, both physical and emotional.

One hour.

For one hour, the women sat on that bench, hands held tight, conversation sporadic, the sea air breathed in deeply as they took in the world around them.

"How are you . . . where you are?" Zara asked, her eyes dipping to her feet.

"Confidence, child," Sister Crow scolded. "Speak your thoughts with assertion. Your curiosity is harmless, and your thoughts are your right."

Zara nodded, drawing a deep breath and trying again. "Why are you homeless? Who are you?"

"Sister Crow," she said, her mouth drawing into a tight line. "The kids, they all call me that because o' my treasures." Sister Crow nodded back toward the shopping cart nestled in an overgrown corner of the boardwalk. "I love the world and all its beauty. The discarded lipstick tubes, the foil wrappers, the coins, the hair." Sister Crow shrugged her shoulders. "A crow, you see."

Zara nodded.

"Garbage, though," Zara mumbled, taking care to keep her eyes elevated.

"Life," Sister Crow retorted. "It's all life."

"No, she's right," Dharius hissed in Sister Crow's ear. "Garbage. You, your life, everything you've done, or rather failed to do."

Sister Crow jolted, swatting at her shoulder and muttering profanities to the empty air.

"You disgust her," Dharius continued. "You are so far beneath anyone and anything, you filthy sow."

"Shut it, you bugger," Sister Crow groaned.

Zara furrowed her brow, looking across Sister Crow to the offending patch of nothing above her shoulder.

Cue the faerie, who quickly put an end to the debasement, using her flaming red hair to bind and gag Dharius and throw him to the ground. The little demon writhed and contorted, the faerie's crimson tresses flowing out of his ears and nose as she dominated him. Sister Crow looked at the pinned devil and the silver faerie sitting cross-legged on his belly, her silver head bobbing to some catchy tune within her own skull. Sister Crow looked back over at Zara, whose face had gone from pink-tinged ivory to ashen gray.

"Ah, sorry," Sister Crow said. "Schizophrenia."

Zara said nothing. She reached out and took Sister Crow's hand, letting their intertwined fingers rest once again across their thighs. The sparkle of a tear swelled across Sister Crow's vision, glistening off the silver flesh of her faerie. She let the tear trickle down her wrinkled cheek. *Emotion is so beautiful and powerful*, she thought, making no move to hide her tear.

"So why are *you* here?" Sister Crow asked.

"I work down the street in the old Strathcona building."

"Boring," Sister Crow snipped. "I mean, why are you in this place in your life? How did you become a defeated slip of a woman, blind to the beauty of life, skulking through your day looking for an end like a character in a side-scrolling video game?"

Zara gasped, offended. She opened her mouth to argue, to quip a retort, but remained silent. She had been hit by the truth, but not blindsided by it. She turned her head and faced the sea. The whisper of the waves rolling against the pier filled her ears, accentuated by the song of gulls seeking treasures, the likes of which Sister Crow would covet. She pictured those gulls flying across the sea to distant shores, free of the dust of this life—free of hurt and pain, doubt and worry.

"Sometimes I wish I could fly," Zara said. "Take to the wind, cross the bay, and start anew. Let my journey across the sea cleanse the rottenness that blinds me and the sludge that weighs me down. Lighten my wings and clear my mind."

Despite her new awareness of her submissive posturing, Zara allowed her eyes to examine her shoes once again. "But I fear that even if I did, nothing would change. Or it would change for the worse. I am who I am, and that's something I cannot go back from."

Sister Crow sat in quiet contemplation for a moment before placing her other hand on Zara's back.

"I wish you could see yourself through my eyes," Sister Crow said.

"You don't know me," Zara said, her brief euphoria of escapism dissipating.

"I know you," Sister Crow said. "I refuse to wallow, so I see things, notice things. I am so little and have so little," Sister Crow winced and glanced down at the venomous demon tethered to the concrete, "that I find beauty in less."

Zara's cellphone shouted at her. She dropped Sister Crow's hand and pulled the vibrating social tether from her pocket.

"Oh, shit," Zara grumbled. "I'm late."

She looked toward Sister Crow without really seeing her and dashed from the bench.

"It was nice meeting you," Zara called back over her shoulder as she sprinted up to the street.

Sister Crow grimaced as her new friend became blind once again.

It should be okay, right?

I nailed the presentation. I deserve a celebration. So this is fine, right?

Zara worried her fingers through the tips of her hair, twitching at each and every little noise: the clink of a glass, an explosion of laughter, the bang of a pint set down on a heavy wooden table.

The day had gone well. So well, in fact, that her coworkers had insisted they all go out for celebratory beverages at the pub around the corner. Zara had begrudgingly obliged. A part of her, hidden way down at the tip of her pinky toe, enjoyed the revelry, the social interaction, the camaraderie. But the majority of her buckled in fear, knowing the impending consequences for her blatant change in routine.

She had called him, several times, but he often left his phone in another room or in a coat pocket. She hadn't come home after work, and her plans had not been previously discussed. And now she was late. Very late. And her phone was dead.

And so am I, she thought.

She feigned interest in the conversations filling the stale pub air, wanting so badly to fit in, to enjoy herself, to forget the reality lurking beyond the pub doors. Out in the night, another world waited for her behind a door a mere twenty blocks from where she sat: a world filled with tears, fists, blood, and a vicious tongue. She wrung her hands together beneath the table, attempting to massage her nagging anxiety into submission. She could still feel her: Sister Crow, the firmness of her grasp and her beautiful outlook on life. Zara closed her eyes and pictured Sister Crow's face, the brightness in her eyes, the colors of the world gravitating to her happiness.

Zara smiled and took a sip of her drink.

One drink turned to many, sitting rose to dancing, and conversation lifted to song and raucous laughter. As one day stumbled into the next, the herd thinned, leaving Zara and a few stragglers to be flushed out into the night come closing time. The remainder of her crew boarded the metro or taxis, but Zara opted to hoof it home. She needed fresh air and time to clear her head before entering the den of the beast.

"You sure you don't want to jump in? We can easily swing by your place. No trouble at all."

Scott, the effeminate IT support guy with his red hair and pale skin, was anything but threatening, and was certainly soothing, but she needed the walk to get herself together.

"No, thanks, Scott," she said.

"You know . . ." Scott said, his voice trailing off.

Zara noticed his eyes flicker briefly to the swelling of her lip, and pity flavored his expression. Her eyes sought her shoes for solace as she waved her hand dismissively in his direction.

"Good night, Scott."

He paused, giving her one last look before his taxi whisked him away into the night.

Zara walked down the street, retracing her steps to the boardwalk where she had sat with Sister Crow in the morning sun, staring out over the ocean. She slowed at their bench, pausing to look out over the glassy water. She thought of Sister Crow and of the distant shores that haunted her desires.

"Who is he?"

Zara spun around and was caught off guard by an explosive-looking Brent, his fists balled and face red.

"Brent, I—"

"You what? Are screwing around on me with that *ginger*?"

She looked at the bench, then directly into Brent's eyes.

"I went out for drinks. After work. We had a good day, we nailed the contract, and we went out to celebrate."

She stood tall. She did not look at her feet.

"I tried to call," she explained.

Sweat beaded on his brow.

"I'm sorry, sweetheart," Zara sighed.

Then, for the second time during those waking hours, Zara tasted her own blood.

"No!" Sister Crow yelped in a stifled scream.

She peered from her hidey-hole as the brute put his hands on her beautiful, damaged friend. As he forcefully exerted his perceived entitlement, Sister Crow turned her head to look away.

"You were nothing to her, anyway," Dharius whispered, licking the inside of her ear with his forked tongue. "You are just a slob, a waste of human flesh taking up real estate on a planet meant for beings with purpose."

The faerie lashed out, attempting to silence the micro-devil with a slash of her tail, but he put up a fight. He wrapped his tiny red talons around her silver neck. She responded by thrusting her golden tongue down his throat, protecting Sister Crow from his wretched commentary. Sister Crow watched as the little folks fought, silvery skin chafing against black, leathery scales, both sets of eyes glowing with passionate determination. The faerie could have overcome the little devil, but instead she thrust out a silvery finger, casting a crystalized light across the street toward the sparring couple. Sister Crow's eyes followed the trail of light, her vision reaching the scene the very moment Zara was midfall. In slow motion, with the little devil cheering and taunting through what sounded like an ocean of molasses, Zara's head struck the bench where they had sat, where they had held hands, and where the world had stopped for a spell. And now that world was still and quiet, save the sound of the whispering waves and the thump of Sister Crow's breaking heart.

Sister Crow didn't hesitate. She loped down the seawall, brandishing little more than Ol' Pinky as a weapon, pushing forward until the palms of her wise and weathered hands met the brute's chest.

"You pig!" she screamed. "You pathetic coward!"

She pounded his chest and clawed at his face, tearing flesh wherever her nails caught purchase. Her hair flailed around her head like the manic snakes of Medusa, and spittle flew from her chapped lips. She became more beast than woman, more volatile than her personal little devil, but she was no match for a male so many years her junior. She felt it in every punch of his fist, every kick of his boot. As her head came to rest on the salty pavement, she couldn't help but wonder at how beautiful the stars were in the night sky.

The stars were still there when Sister Crow opened her eyes. They still shone brightly, the moon still high in the sky.

"Hrmph," she groaned. "Mus' still be nighttime."

She didn't know how long she had been out, but it couldn't have been too great a time if the night was in full bloom. The bastard had pummeled her after 2 a.m., and the sun's alarm rang at 6, so she was somewhere in between. She turned her head and saw Zara lying facedown in front of the bench, blood pooling beneath the stream trickling from her lips. Zara's chest heaved, slightly and slowly, but enough to show she still drew breath.

"Good girl. Stay strong."

Sister Crow used her hands to grope her own body, searching for what might be out of place and waiting to hinder her effort. *Everything*, she concluded. Pangs of pain shot through her broken body, and there were spears of bone where bone should not have been. "Ah, well. I was becomin' obsolete, anyway." *That one, though* . . . She looked over at Zara.

Using every ounce of fortitude in her mind, body, and soul, Sister Crow struggled to her knees, then to her haunches, and finally hoisted herself to her feet. She walked over to the bench and cringed as she dropped back down to the ground.

"Girl, I'm gonna touch you, okay?"

Sister Crow ran her hands along Zara's body, relieved to find her relatively intact. Aside from a likely concussion, the brute had inflicted some superficial bruising and emotional heartache, but not much more. Sister Crow got to her feet again and walked to her cart. The faerie was perched in a nearby tree, still and silent, breathless in anticipation.

"Okay, little one. Let's get to work."

Red kissed the morning sky, casting a pink glow over the lazy fog lingering over the water. Zara woke to pain and confusion. Her vision was milky, and her tongue pasty and dry. Her head pounded a dull, steady waltz.

Brent.

She sat up and pressed her hand against her chest, sighing in relief at the beat against her palm.

Okay. I'm alive.

She touched her head and found one hell of a goose egg perched on her temple. Her body ached, and she cringed against abrasions on her knees and arms. Thankfully, someone had covered her in a pink blanket that sheltered her from the crisp sea air. She pulled off the blanket and looked down at her blouse, expecting additional blood on the already-stained outfit. There was more blood, yes, and a lot of it. But over the blood, fastened to her blouse by safety pins and scotch tape, were pieces of garbage—flyers, wrappers, discarded scraps of fabric, feathers—cut into all manner of shapes. Hearts, stars, snowflakes. She stared at the adornments, seeing them more as decorations than garbage. Shiny foil, vibrant colors, precisely constructed art. And her skin, a pallid ivory, bruised and tainted, was scripted with dozens of messages scrawled in paint and food and fluids of questionable origins.

You are beautiful.

You are more than this.

You are not trapped.

You are powerful.

You belong only to yourself.

You are a part of the world, and you have use. Beauty. Emotion. Purpose.

Be you.

Be free.

Fly.

Zara frantically scanned the area, and she saw it, in a nook tucked away at the end of the boardwalk behind a bush ripe with flowers. Feet, bloodied and contorted at unnatural angles, peeking out from behind their floral blind.

"Oh!" Zara exclaimed.

She stood, her legs realizing they must carry her weight. She hobbled over to the bush and swiped away the brambles, revealing her now-broken friend.

"Sister Crow," Zara said, tears spilling from her swollen eyes.

Sister Crow tried to sit up, but her body wouldn't comply, leaving her limp and sputtering on the ground.

"Ah, it's no odds, child," Sister Crow sputtered as she raised a hand to Zara's cheek.

Zara fumbled for her pockets and then glanced at the bench where her purse lay. She moved to stand, but Sister Crow stopped her and clasped her hand against her breast.

"Let me call an ambulance," Zara pleaded. "The police."

"It's my end, child," Sister Crow said, a weak smile on her face. "He done me good. But it's my time. I have no fear or regret. Life has been good and beautiful and kind. And long enough."

Sister Crow's eyes drifted from Zara's face, following the glowing light over her shoulder. The faerie was there, a beacon against the backdrop of crimson sky, her gleaming, glittering skin sending the rising sun pirouetting in lyrical prisms.

"He did this," Zara said on feeble breath.

"He did," Sister Crow said.

"You tried to stop him. To save me."

"I did."

They were quiet. They held hands and smiled until the bustle of routine ignited on the street behind the boardwalk.

"I can't leave you here like this," Zara whispered, her lower lip quavering.

"You can, and you will," Sister Crow said, smiling at the faerie dancing around them in the air, encasing them in a cocoon of iridescent light strands. "Don't worry. I'm not alone."

Zara let herself cry, moistening her friend in a heartfelt tear-bath that cleansed them both. Zara pried Sister Crow's hand from hers and retrieved Ol' Pinky from the bench. She returned the blanket to Sister Crow, drawing it over her battered body and up to her chin. Sister Crow squealed and hugged into the blanket, nuzzling her face into its familiar embrace.

Zara went to stand, and Sister Crow grabbed her arm.

"And what of you?" Sister Crow asked. The faerie's glow faded, waiting for the answer.

Zara thought, though the decision had already cemented itself in her heart. She looked at her body, the beautiful disaster of garbage, the messages of love and hope, and turned her eyes to the sea.

"Good," Sister Crow said. "Very good, then."

"But he can't get away with this," Zara said.

"He won't," Sister Crow said. "It will weigh on him, the viciousness, his loss. It will eat him like a bucket o' maggots wedged into his guts."

Zara looked unsure.

"That," Sister Crow said, a wicked smile stretching her lips, "and I got a piece o' him. A wee souvenir for the cops when they find me."

She held up her hand, and Zara saw that her long nails were bloodied, strips of flesh and clumps of hair embedded deep under her yellowed claws. And most importantly, the tattered leather wallet clutched in Sister Crow's bony grasp.

Zara smiled.

She knelt down and kissed the old woman on the forehead, and they held each other's faces for a long moment before Zara walked away.

Sister Crow watched as the no-longer-defeated woman walked away. She watched as a ticket was purchased and those scuffed shoes left the dock.

"Good," Sister Crow said, heavy sobs creeping out between shallow breaths.

Sister Crow felt a soft hand against her cheek. The faerie was there, stroking her skin, bright aqua tears of joy twinkling in her crystal eyes. Sister Crow looked from side to side, seeking the faerie's adversary, but Dharius was nowhere to be found.

The faerie extended a long, floating finger, tapping Sister Crow on the chest. For the first time, the faerie opened her mouth and spoke. The word was musical, a beautiful note that resonated clear through to Sister Crow's soul.

"Hero."

The world crumbled into a kaleidoscope of color and then faded to silver, brighter, brighter . . .

And Sister Crow smiled.

Zara imagined Sister Crow's hand. She felt it upon her own as she purchased her ticket to board the ferry, as she stepped aboard the empty boat, and as she pulled away from shore, heading to the great unknown. She could feel her friend's hand upon her face as she looked up at the sky, the warmth of the sun soothing her healing skin. Zara had nothing, but she had everything. She had no belongings, no immediate plans; nothing but the clothes on her back and the purse on her arm. But she had hope. She had a future.

She had a new start.

She walked to the bow of the boat and gazed out across the open water, imagining her first step on her next shore. She closed her eyes.

And she flew.

LITTLE AVA SAVES THE WORLD
VERSTANDT

The warm summer sunshine poured through the living room window, casting a soft glow across little Ava Oswald. She sat cross-legged in front of the television with her head resting in the palms of her hands. A small blanket, tied loosely at her neck, served as a cape, and atop her head sat a paper crown crudely fashioned after the attire of Princess Stupendous.

Beside her sat her best and only friend. The short hair of his arm bristled harshly against the back of her neck, and his cloven hoof sat heavy on her shoulder, but she seemed not to mind.

She watched the television in wide-eyed wonder as Princess Stupendous battled the evil Baron Skulgor and his hordes of snaggle-toothed minions.

When the goat spoke, the tenor of his voice resonated with a subtle vibrato, as if his words passed through the thin hair of a violin's bow. He said to her, "The Greenland shark lives deep, deep under the ocean where all is cold and dark. His vision is very dim from living in such a dark place for the whole of his life."

"Uh-huh," she said, her eyes never leaving the epic battle before her.

"But every once in a while, Ava, he rises. He never makes his way as far up as the surface, but he makes it far enough to see the light, if only for a few moments."

As Princess Stupendous vanquished the waves of minions and Baron Skulgor slipped away into the wood, Ava finally pulled her gaze from the screen. She looked up into the bulbous eyes of the goat and said, "Baff, when I grow up, I want to be a superhero just like Princess Stupendous."

"You will," he said. "Someday very soon you are going to save the whole world."

"I am?" she asked.

Just then, her mother walked into the room, her eyes dark and tears still wet on her cheeks.

"You are what, sweetie?" her mother asked.

"Tell your mother I love her very much," the goat said.

"Baff says he loves you very much, Mommy," Ava said.

"Well, you tell Baff I love him, too, but not as much as I love you." She knelt down and swept Ava up into her arms and hugged her tight, and her tears mingled with her daughter's hair.

She finally set her daughter down and wiped the tears from her eyes.

"Are we going to go see Grammy today?" Ava asked.

"Yes, we are, sweetness, and we need to get going. Go grab your things."

Ava's mother strapped her into the backseat of the car and tugged at the seatbelt to make sure it was secure. She brushed the hair out of her eyes and shut the door. Baff sat silently beside Ava.

As they drove, she watched out the window at the passing cars and scenery as Baff spoke.

"There is a parasite that lives deep, deep in the ocean with the Greenland shark," he said. "It has but one source of food in all the great wide ocean. It seeks out and attaches itself to the eyes of the Greenland shark, and it never, ever let's go."

Ava stood in the gift shop attached to the hospital lobby, haloed on all sides by wilted and dying flowers. Baff stood silently beside her.

Her mother's voice, teetering on the edge of hysterics, argued with the store clerk at the counter. The young man wore a doe-eyed pleading expression.

"It's a hospital. You would think you would have some flowers that weren't right on the edge of death."

"I'm sorry, ma'am, but I just don't have any control over the flowers we have," the clerk responded.

"Jesus, are you all just completely helpless about what happens in your own damn store? I mean, who is responsible for anything around here?"

Ava tuned all of this out and sifted through the multitudes of floral arrangements on display. Her eyes passed over dandelions and roses, daffodils and carnations, chrysanthemums and orchids, but not a single lily in the entire display. Each of them drooped, and their petals were tinged with encroaching decay.

Then her gaze fell upon an arrangement of sunflowers. They were a sad sight with their heads hanging heavy like men heading solemnly to the gallows.

She approached these sullen flowers, and though they reeked of entropy, she was mesmerized by the boldness of their stalks, and the rich yellows that still clung to the base of each petal.

Baff said, "The Ommatokoita parasite eats at the eyes of the Greenland shark until it has devoured all of what little sight he was blessed with. And then he spends the rest of his centuries of life utterly blind and alone in the coldest depths of the ocean."

Ava reached out one tiny hand and brushed her fingers across the sunflower's petals. They raised their weary heads. Their wilt receded, and the scent of their decay fell away.

She took the flowers into her arms and marched them to the front counter, where her mother and the cashier argued. She raised them high and said, "Will these work, Mommy?"

They both turned and stared, their argument abruptly halted as they were caught in a momentary muted awe at the glowing and resplendent display. Ava's mother thanked her daughter and hastily paid the $14.95 for the arrangement. She took her daughter by the hand and led her out of the hospital gift shop. Baff followed after.

The sunflowers rested forgotten on a table next to a screened window. Ava sat quietly in the small hospital room beside her mother, who held her Grammy's hand. Her Grammy's eyes were closed, her face ashen, her hand unresponsive. All about her was the gentle cacophony of rubber soles tapping against linoleum, the ringing of phones, and muted chatter. There were the beeps and whirring hums of the machines hooked into her Grammy. There were the soft sobs of her mother. All these sounds merged into a whispered hum that was soothing in its monotony.

She watched in hypnotic fascination as Baff poked his nose around the various electronic machines that sat next to the bed. She opened her mouth to ask him what he was doing, but just then he turned to her and placed a hoof to his mouth. She halted the words in her throat and swallowed them back down into her belly. Then he pointed and said, "Look, Ava, there are flies on the windscreen."

She got up and walked over to the window and saw that there were indeed three dead flies upon it, two of them lying on the sill and one hanging with its leg caught in the screen. Ava wrinkled her nose. She extended one finger and poked at the dangling fly. Its wings twitched once and then were still. Then its legs twitched and were still once again. Then it came violently alive, frantically thrashing about, trying to free itself from the trap of the screen. Finally, it managed to pull its leg free, and it flew up into the room, buzzing about freely in wide, meandering loops and dives. Ava watched this with a barely perceptible smile upon her face.

As Ava watched the fly do its dance around the room, a large woman dressed in blue scrubs and brandishing a clipboard burst into the room. Baff ceased his investigations and backed quietly into a corner.

"How are we doing today, Ms. Oswald?"

Ava's mother looked up at the nurse and forced a weary smile.

"I'm doing fine, Norma. How are you?"

"Well, I'm just peachy." She knelt in front of Ava.

"How are we today, little Miss Ava?"

"Fine," Ava said, wriggling her hands and squirming her way into her mother's arms.

"Well, that's just fine. And how is Gramma Oswald doing today?"

"The same. She hasn't stirred at all."

"Well, that's . . ." She halted as the fly buzzed directly past her gaze. All three of them watched as the fly took one loop around her head and then landed on the foot of the bed.

The clipboard came crashing down. The nurse was fast, and her aim was true. The fly bounced once on the bed and fell dead to the floor. They all stared wordlessly at it for a moment. Then Ava harrumphed, crossed her arms, and stuck her bottom lip out at the nurse. The nurse didn't notice.

"I'm awfully sorry about that," the nurse said. "The summertime brings them, you know. We do what we can to stave them off, but good ol' Mother Nature, well, she just finds a way, don't she?"

"Yes, I suppose she does," Ava's mother said.

"Ms. Oswald, I was wondering if I might have a moment in private."

Fear tinged the edges of Ava's mother's eyes, but she acquiesced. "Yes, of course." They stepped into the hallway, and Ava was left alone with Baff and her Grammy.

Baff made his way back to the equipment and recommenced his investigations. Ava approached her Grammy. She watched her Grammy's eyes dance back and forth beneath the thin veil of her lids. Her sickly pungent breath passed thinly through parted lips, and though the room was cool, a sheen of sweat enveloped her features. Ava slipped her hands into her Grammy's, and her Grammy's eyes fluttered briefly and slowly opened. Grammy turned her head to the side and saw her granddaughter. A wan smile fell across her face like a fallen scarf.

"Hello, Grammy."

"Hello, my love." Her voice was hoarse, little more than a rasp, but in it was an abundance of gentleness.

"Grammy, you smell funny."

Grammy laughed weakly. "I know, dear. I'm sorry."

"Grammy, when are you going to take me fishing again?"

"Oh, honey, I think my fishing days are over."

"Are you dying, Grammy?"

"Yes, dear, I think I am."

"Does it hurt?"

"Only when I'm awake. But when I sleep, I go to a wonderful, happy place. And your grandpa is there with me, and we are very happy." She tightened her grip on Ava's hand and looked fiercely at her. "So I don't want you to be frightened for me or sad for me or scared when your time comes. Okay? Can you do that for me, my love?"

"Yes, ma'am."

"Good, good." Her grip loosened, and her head rested easily on her pillow.

"Is Daddy there, too?"

"Yes, honey, your daddy is there, too. Now, I want you to do something for me, okay, dear?"

"Yes, Grammy?"

"I want you to let me go back to sleep."

"Yes, Grammy," she said and pulled her hand away.

"I love you, Ava," her Grammy whispered as her eyes slipped closed and resumed their dance beneath her lids.

Baff stepped forward and stood across from Ava, his hooves resting on the opposite side of her Grammy's bed. He said, "The common ant spends the entirety of his life in service to his queen and to his colony. He works tirelessly, day and night, performing tasks of the most grueling labor. His loyalty, through all of his hardships and suffering, never once waivers."

Ava looked over at the dead fly lying on the floor and wondered if he was in the fly Happy Place, fishing eternity away with all his fly friends and loved ones.

It was at that moment that the heart monitor attached to her Grammy's chest rang out its high-pitched, tuneless song.

The ride home was a wordless one on the parts of both Ava and her mother. The music of Vivaldi's *Four Seasons* drifted unheard through the car. Ava watched life continue, unperturbed by her Grammy's passing, on the other side the car window. In the seat beside her, Baff spoke softly.

"There is a fungus of the genus *Ophiocordyceps* that infects the common ant. It spreads rapidly through his body, his central nervous system, and finally his brain. It takes over the will of the ant. It forces him to climb high up onto a branch overlooking his colony and latch on. That branch is where he will spend the last few moments of his life."

Ava sat with her hand in her mother's, fighting with every ounce of her will to refrain from squirming. The pew beneath her was hard, and the preacher's voice was eternally long and droning. What few friends and relatives had deigned to attend the service sat scattered among the pews. Each awkward shift, each muffled sniffle, each hushed reproach to a disobedient child seemed a minute refrain to the sanctity of the memorial. The stifling formality of the service was nearly more than Ava could bear.

She looked to Baff, and he looked back at her. He said, "The fungus that infects the ant, it eventually shatters the skull of the ant, killing him. It grows a long, long stalk out of the top of the ant's head. Once it gets long enough, it erupts, raining hundreds of spores down upon the colony, dooming each of his brethren to the same fate."

The sermon eventually wound to a close, and the congregation formed a short line before the casket. Ava and her mother stood right at the front of this line, as if at the head of a morbid game of Follow the Leader.

They slowly approached and beheld the lifeless thing that had been her Grammy. Ava's mother broke down into hysterical sobs, nearly falling to the floor. The preacher ushered her away, but Ava stayed, and as always, Baff stood by her side. The face that lay in the casket was but a pale mockery of the smiling eyes and glowing cheeks that her grandmother had once possessed. These features had been replaced by thickly caked blush, base, and mascara, applied as with a palette knife. Still, it was her Grammy's face, and Ava could sense a spark still there. She slowly reached her hand into the casket and stretched her fingers out toward the pale cheek of her grandmother. Then she was halted by a cloven hoof upon her shoulder.

"No," Baff said.

She looked up at him, bewilderment in her eyes. "But . . ."

He shook his head and tapped his hoof to his mouth.

She silenced, and he said, "Remember what your Grammy told you. She's in the Happy Place now. Come along, it's time to go."

Ava followed him away and returned to her place in the pews next to her mother, who sat crying with her head upon the preacher's shoulder.

Ten days had run their course since her Grammy's passing. Her meager possessions from the hospital lay forgotten on the kitchen counter, including the sunflowers, now withered black and dead. Little Ava Oswald sat cross-legged in her living room in front of the television. The milk in the refrigerator had turned rancid and clumpy, so she shoveled dry cereal into her mouth with a spoon. Her construction paper crown sat askew atop a greasy rat's nest of hair, and dandruff coated the shoulders of her cape. Baff sat silently beside her.

On the screen, Princess Stupendous was once again battling the evil Baron Skulgor and his seething minions. As Princess Stupendous chased the Baron Skulgor from the Rainbow Castle of Ever-Present Love and Light, Ava turned to Baff. "Do you think Mommy is ever going to come out?"

"Why don't you ask her?"

Ava set her bowl down, got up, and made her way down the hall. She came to her mother's bedroom door and slowly swung it open. Inside, the curtains were drawn and the room was dark. The damp reek of booze permeated the room. Her mother lay facedown, splayed across the bed.

Ava called softly, "Mommy, are you awake?"

"Go away, Ava. Mommy is sleeping." Her mother's voice was deep and sluggish.

"Mommy, when are you getting up?"

"Later. Go and play. Mommy will be up later."

"Are you sad, Mommy?"

"I said, go and play."

She closed the door as silently as she could and looked up at Baff.

"What do we do?" she asked.

"We do as she said. We go and play."

Ava ran, weaving through the woods behind her house with her arms spread out on either side of her like an airplane. Her cape flapped in the wind, leaves swirled in the eddies of her wake, and her crown held to the top of her head by some miracle of the gods. Baff ran effortlessly beside her. As they ran Baff said, "There is a forest in Japan, on the far side of Mount Fuji. The whole of the forest resides atop a hardened layer of lava. It is known as Aokigahara, the Sea of Trees."

Ava finally slowed, panting and out of breath, and they continued their journey at a casual walk.

"The hardened lava the forest resides upon is very porous. It absorbs all sound and gives the woods a nearly otherworldly serenity. It is an exceptionally peaceful place to be. There are signs posted all about the edges of the forest, urging those who visit to turn away."

As they walked, they came to a small clearing. In the center of the clearing lay a rabbit.

"The forest has another name, and it's where people go in search of the Happy Place. You have to wonder if those trees don't feel sorrow."

They knelt before the rabbit. Red blood spotted its white fur. One leg was twisted and broken. Some animal had targeted it as prey or play.

"What do you want to be, Ava?" Baff asked.

"I want to be a superhero, like Princess Stupendous."

Ava reached out and brushed her fingers across the rabbit's fur. Its legs trembled, its nostrils flared and its eyes flew open.

"Remember what happened to the fly," Baff said.

The rabbit stood and looked about in a daze.

"Remember the flowers," Baff said.

The rabbit bolted toward the tree line at the edge of the clearing.

"Remember the Greenland shark and the loyal ant."

The rabbit was but yards away from the edge of the clearing when it stopped. Its nose twitched suspiciously at the air.

"Remember all of this, Ava, and watch."

A wolf stepped from behind the tree line and into the clearing. Its fur was black as plague. Its head hung low—a creature on the hunt. Its lips parted into a grim, hungry smile. Its eyes locked, unwavering, on the rabbit.

The wolf pounced. The rabbit was swift, but not swift enough. The wolf snatched it up and shook it viciously. Fresh blood splashed across the clearing. Ava screamed, and the beast ceased its thrashing. It dropped its prey and swung it eyes to Ava. Her scream died in her throat.

"Princess Stupendous has a sword with which to vanquish evil. You do not. But you need not be afraid. Take my hoof, Ava."

Ava took Baff's hoof in her hand, and together they stepped forward. The wolf laid its ears against its skull. They took another step forward, and the wolf stepped back. Then they were walking, almost casually, toward the beast. It snarled once, then turned and ran away.

They approached the rabbit. It was screaming, a piercing squeal of pure agony, terror, and dismay, and Ava's eyes welled with tears and spilled streams down her face.

"You don't have to be Princess Stupendous. You have another power, untapped and greater than the sword of Princess Stupendous," Baff said. "You can be your own superhero, with your own superpower. What is it you really want your power to be?"

"I want to make people happy."

"Then remember the Sea of Trees. Don't make it go through this again. Send it to the Happy Place instead, Ava," he said and gestured toward the rabbit with a smile.

Ava reached out toward the rabbit. Its eyes closed, its breathing slowed, and finally it was still.

She looked up at Baff and said, "The rabbit is with Grammy now?"

"Yes, it's with Grammy, in the Happy Place. You can dry your tears now."

Ava sniffled and ran her cheeks along her sleeve. They stood and looked about and saw that the sky had turned the color of a bruise. Dusk had arrived. Baff said, "Let's go home."

The room was nearly pitch black. The heavy stench of old sweat and booze was overwhelmingly oppressive. Ava stood beside the bed, Baff directly behind her. Her mother twisted and turned in restless, fitful sleep.

"Remember the rabbit," Baff said.

"She'll be happy with Grammy?" Ava whispered.

"Who wouldn't be happy with Grammy?" Baff replied.

Ava reached out her hand.

When it was done, Baff whispered a single word. "Matricide."

"What?" Ava asked.

"Nothing, Ava. Come along. It's time to save the world."

He left the room, and Ava followed after.

Little Ava Oswald, wearing a cape fashioned from a blanket and a crown fashioned from construction paper, walked down the middle of a suburban road. She leaned her head back and closed her eyes. Her arms were outstretched, her fingers splayed and pointing toward the edges of the world. Beside her walked her best and only friend, Baff. All throughout the world, people's eyelids became heavy and their breathing became shallow and slow. In China, children laid their weary heads down in school hallways. In Germany, factory workers laid down on factory floors. In all the world, every living man, woman, and child slumbered as she sent them all to that eternal Happy Place.

All the fishes of all the oceans and all the lakes and all the rivers slipped into silent and eternal slumber.

All the birds fell from the sky, and all the insects of the world fell silent.

Little Ava Oswald had become Death.

When all living things had fallen to slumber, Ava and Baff wandered through the dark with no place to go. Eventually, they stopped and sat with their backs against the cold brick wall of an abandoned convenience store.

Baff looked up to the night sky and said, "They will all be lonely without the stars."

Ava looked up, and stars blinked out, one by one. The light of the moon was the last to go.

It was cold, and it was dark, and Ava sat alone with Baff. Ice had formed across her cheek, her brow, and her fingers. If there had been light to see by, her lips would have been blue. Her cape had come loose and fallen to the ground beside her. She turned to Baff and said, "My hands are cold. Can you tie my cape?"

Baff clapped his hooves together and said, "I can't."

They were quiet for a while, save for Ava's chattering teeth.

Finally, Baff said, "I am proud of you, Ava."

She smiled weakly and guessed that all things must be happy now, except for her, for she was all alone.

"Can I go to sleep now, Baff?" she asked.

"Yes, you can sleep now."

Ava closed her eyes and slipped into slumber, satisfied that she had saved the world.

Baff sat silently beside her.

ABOUT THE COVER ARTIST

Verstandt R. A. Shelton is Inklings Publishing's cover artist.
Growing up as a childhood misfit, Verstandt R. A. Shelton wiled
away the hours daydreaming of floating in space and sitting at the
bottom of the ocean floor. A disquieting obsession for the less
beaten paths of philosophical ponderings and environmental
extremes led him to stumble into the murky depths of the writerly
craft. You can find him today chained in the back of his closet with
the lights out, a bottle of whiskey in hand, and the ghosts of his
inspirations (Stephen King, Clive Barker, Milton, Lovecraft, and
Dante) breathing down his neck, writing stories to terrify the world.
His lovely wife, Jennifer, and his cat, Siouxsie Q, worry for his safety.

ABOUT THE AUTHORS

Emerson Adair is a Texas resident who loves stories. Sharing tales, whether they spring from real experiences or flights of fancy, is a passion she developed from her childhood, when her father read her fairy tales by the fireplace. She worked for seven years at a small-town newspaper in the Coastal Bend area and now works to promote higher education in the area.

Adam Carlson is a stay-at-home dad who spends his idle time writing (mostly when the kids are napping). "PR" is the first story he has published, but hopefully not the last.

Cathy Clay is a native Houstonian. She earned a bachelor's degree in creative writing from the University of Houston in 1997 and a master's degree in English from Texas Southern University in 2008. Her debut novel, *Agatta*, was published in 2010. Her short stories "Cecil" and "The Earrings" appear respectively in *Eclectically Criminal* and *Eclectically Cosmic*. Her poems can be found in *Two Cities Review* ("Sabotage of Innocence"), *Chest Journal* ("On the Mend"), and *Rat's Ass Review* ("Hiss"). In addition to writing, she enjoys family, animals, and the arts.

Kelly Lynn Colby is a professional volunteer, fledgling writer, and hardcore geek. She volunteers with the Girl Scouts and Boy Scouts, as well as the high school her son attends and the farm where her daughter learns equestrian skills. She has joined Inklings Publishing as both an acquisitions editor and a developmental editor. Her epic fantasy, Tarbin's True Heir, just released in September 2017. When she is not attending to her myriad duties, Kelly enjoys reading and traveling, especially to Sci-Fi conventions, such as Dragon Con.

Kelsey Dean currently lives in Seoul, where she teaches English, writes, and paints. Her fiction and poetry have appeared or are forthcoming in a variety of publications, including *The Binge-Watching Cure*, *Cast of Wonders*, *Liminal Stories*, and *Cicada*, among others. Her

YA short story "Starfishing" is available on Audible.com, and she occasionally blogs at http://kelseypaints.tumblr.com.

Sir Andross Draneg was born on the planet Jorn in the city Dran on his father's prosperous farm. During the war before unification on Jorn, Andross proved himself such a worthy warrior that he was knighted. In service to King Amiel and Queen Verena, Sir Andross was often sent on a variety of missions. Thanks to these, he collected notebooks full of myths, legends, and other assorted tales from the peoples of Thyrein's Galactic Wall. Having found his journals, Fern Brady has taken it upon herself to bring these well-written stories to the readers of Earth.

Darrel Duckworth returned to his first love, writing, after a career in high tech. He now spends more time on other worlds, occasionally returning to Earth to refill his coffee mug. His stories can be found in magazines such as *LORE*, *Bards and Sages*, and *Plasma Frequency* and in anthologies such as *Coven* and *Wild Things*.

Jim Horlock is descended from Viking warriors on one side and Celtic witches on the other. He has a great passion for storytelling and an obsession with tropes, which often leads to him working out the ends of films within the first ten minutes, much to the annoyance of his friends. He loves horror movies, video games, table-top RPGs, board games, and comic books. He is largely carnivorous. He has a degree in creative and professional writing from the University of Glamorgan in South Wales. Now if only he could remember where he put it.

Jae Mazer is a Canadian who was born in Victoria, British Columbia, and grew up on the prairies of Northern Alberta. After spending the majority of her life in the Great White North, she migrated south to Texas. Now she enjoys life as a mom, a musician, and a connoisseur and creator of horror, science fiction, and fantasy. Many moons ago, a rampant love of reading led her to believe she could weave a good tale herself, and she now has six novels under her belt. Jae is very excited to be part of the Inklings Publishing family.

Christina Robertson grew up on the north side of Chicago. Her parents, a cartoonist and a part-time PR writer, lived thriftily but exposed her to great books and music. Her curiosity for the darker and more vulnerable sides of people ultimately led her to a degree in psychology and work within clinical settings as a counselor and an art therapist. Today, she lives in Evanston, Illinois, with her restaurateur husband and their teenage daughter. Her short stories have appeared in *The Raven's Perch*, *Midwestern Gothic*, and *The Ponder Review*.

Verstandt R. A. Shelton wiled away his misfit childhood daydreaming of floating in space and sitting on the ocean floor. A disquieting obsession for the less beaten paths of philosophical ponderings and environmental extremes led him to stumble into the murky depths of the writerly craft. You can find him today chained in the back of his closet with the lights out, a bottle of whiskey in hand, and the ghosts of his inspirations (Stephen King, Clive Barker, Milton, Lovecraft, and Dante) breathing down his neck, writing stories to terrify the world. His lovely wife, Jennifer, and his cat, Siouxsie Q, worry for his safety.

Neil Slevin, MA, BSc, is a writer from Co. Leitrim, Ireland. His poetry has been published by various Irish publications, including *The Galway Review*, *A New Ulster*, *Skylight 47*, *Boyne Berries*, and *Into the Void*. It can also be found in numerous international journals, such as *Scarlet Leaf Review* and *Artificium: The Journal*. His flash fiction has appeared in *The Incubator*. Neil is also the founder and editor of *Dodging the Rain*.

Stuart Suffel's body of "work" includes stories published by Meerkat Press, Jurassic London, Evil Girlfriend Media, Enchanted Conversation: A Fairy Tale Magazine, and Aurora Wolf, among others. He exists in Ireland, lives in the Twilight Zone, and will work for Chocolate Sambuca ice cream.

Dorothy Tinker grew up dreaming of fantastical worlds and creatures, of plots in space, and of strange cultures. Two years after being side-tracked by "real life" in the form of a math-based stint at UTD, she rediscovered her true passion and rededicated herself to her literary dreams. Since then, she has published an ongoing series of YA fantasy novels, including *Peace of Evon*, *Gift of War*, and *Lost King*. Her short stories have appeared in HWG Press's *Riding the Waves* and *Out of Many, One*, Inklings Publishing's *Eclectically Cosmic*, and Writespace's *In Medias Res*.

Other Books by
Inklings Publishing &
Inklings Children Division

This epic fantasy novel, *Tarbin's True Heir*, is the first of Kelly Lynn Colby's The Recharging series. Follow a pair of royal twins as they go head-to-head to prove to all peoples which of them, older sister or younger brother, is the True Heir.

THE RECHARGING
BOOK ONE

TARBIN'S
TRUE
HEIR

KELLY LYNN COLBY

The Twisted Reveries Series by Meg Hafdahl debuted in October 2015 with *Thirteen Tales of the Macabre*. In October 2016, *Tales from Willoughby* followed.

Get your copy of these spine-tingling volumes today and enjoy short stories by this great female voice in horror!

This international legal thriller is the first book in the Roberto Duran series. Get to know this intrepid criminal attorney from Houston as he fights to uncover the truth and save a young Mexican socialite from wrongful incarceration.

PAYBACK

A ROBERTO DURAN NOVEL

RAMON DEL VILLAR

This bilingual resource provides insight into the workings of a civil lawsuit in terms anyone can understand. Great for interpreters, as well as authors who are writing legal thrillers.

Interpreters'
Anatomy *of a*
Civil Lawsuit

Anatomía *de un*
Juicio Civil *para*
Intérpretes Judiciales

Ramón M. del Villar

Attorney at Law
Federally Certified Court Interpreter
State Licensed Court Interpreter

Licenciado en Derecho
Intérprete Judicial Certificación Federal
Intérprete Judicial Texas, Maestría

Not sure what you're looking for? Pick up an anthology from the Eclectic Writings Series. Each is based on a theme and

features a variety of great authors. This collection is guaranteed to surprise and entertain.

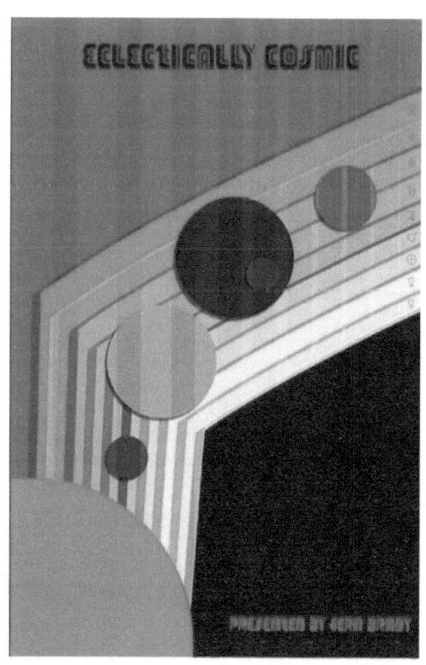

The Smiley Face Blatoon, now available in a bilingual Spanish/English edition, launched Inklings Children Division in Summer 2015. First-place winner of the Texas Authors Association's Best Picture Book for All Ages, this, and all Inklings Children Division books, contains extensive activities, discussion questions, and cross-curricular work, as well as other tools for parents and educators.

The anthologies in the Perceptions Series are collections of short stories, poems, and nonfiction articles based on themes written for children grades three through six by a variety of authors. As with all Inklings Children Division books, each volume contains questions and activities for parents and educators to extend learning.

Perceptions Series
Volume One

Edited by: Fern Brady

Follow Inklings Publishing by:

 Signing up for our newsletter at www.inklingspublishing.com

 Liking our Facebook page

 And following our tweets

www.ingramcontent.com/pod-product-compliance
Lightning Source LLC
Chambersburg PA
CBHW022017170626
46808CB00001B/461